'That's enough of that.' Coop lifted the rum cocktail out of her hand and held it easily out of reach. 'I want you to be able to walk out of here.'

Ella sent him a mock pout, but couldn't disguise her happiness as his gaze settled on her face the way it had been doing all evening—with a gratifying combination of possessiveness and desire.

It was official. Ella's flirt was now fully operational, and the intoxicating buzz of the Rum Swizzle was nothing compared to the glorious buzz of anticipation.

'And where exactly would I be walking to?' She arched her eyebrow, her tone rich with a confidence she'd thought had died inside her a lifetime ago.

His thumb brushed her cheek, his irises a mesmerising moss-green in the bar's half-light. 'My beach hut's down at the other end of the cove. You ready to take a stroll with me in the moonlight?'

The surge of excitement made her giddy. Touching her lips to his, she licked across the seam of the wide sensual mouth that had been driving her wild all day. The shot of power was as stimulating as the pulse of reaction when she heard him drag in a ragged breath.

She let him in, her tongue duelling with his as they sank into a ravenous kiss.

He broke away first, the pants of his breathing as thready as her own. 'I'm gonna take that as a yes.'

Dear Reader

Who *doesn't* love the idea of a wildly romantic, super-sexy holiday fling? You can throw caution to the wind and have the time of your life because the very best thing about it is that he's not going to follow you home...

Um...unless you're my heroine, Ella Radley, who ends up with rather more baggage to unpack than she intended when her holiday fling with studly boat captain Cooper Delaney leaves her with a surprise parting gift. And Cooper? Well, beneath that laid-back, relaxed beach bum charm there's quite a lot of baggage too—but, luckily for him, Ella's just the girl to unpack it for him...whether he wants it unpacked or not.

Now, Ella was a sunny, slightly kooky secondary character in a book I wrote several years ago called CUPCAKES AND KILLER HEELS (available on www.millsandboon.co.uk as an eBook), and readers since have asked me to write her story—which is frankly why she's in this predicament. Poor Coop, though, is just an innocent bystander. Luckily he's not *that* innocent, so I don't think any of us need feel the least bit guilty about putting him through the wringer too.

There is a valuable lesson for us all to learn here: next time you spot some irresistible hunk across a crowded beach bar, who's looking back at you with a matching 'let's get naughty' glint in his eye, just remember that sometimes holiday flings can be too hot to handle!

I love to hear from readers—you can contact me through my website at www.heidi-rice.com

Heidi x

BEACH BAR BABY

BY
HEIDI RICE

Published in Great Britain 2014
by Mills & Boon, an imprint of Harlequin (UK) Limited,
Eton House, 18-24 Paradise Road, Richmond, Surrey, TW9 1SR

© 2014 Heidi Rice

ISBN: 978 0 263 24222 5

Harlequin (UK) Limited's policy is to use papers that are natural,
renewable and recyclable products and made from wood grown in
sustainable forests. The logging and manufacturing processes conform
to the legal environmental regulations of the country of origin.

Printed and bound in Great Britain
by CPI Antony Rowe, Chippenham, Wiltshire

Heidi Rice was born and bred and still lives in London, England. She has two sons who love to bicker, a wonderful husband who, luckily for everyone, has loads of patience, and a supportive and ever-growing British/French/Irish/American family. As much as Heidi adores 'the Big Smoke', she also loves America, and every two years or so she and her best friend leave hubby and kids behind and *Thelma and Louise* it across the States for a couple of weeks (although they always leave out the driving off a cliff bit).

She's been a film buff since her early teens, and a romance junkie for almost as long. She indulged her first love by being a film reviewer for ten years. Then a few years ago she decided to spice up her life by writing romance. Discovering the fantastic sisterhood of romance writers (both published and unpublished) in Britain and America made it a wild and wonderful journey to her first Mills & Boon® novel.

Heidi loves to hear from readers—you can e-mail her at heidi@heidi-rice.com, or visit her website: www.heidi-rice.com

Other Modern Tempted™ titles by Heidi Rice:

MAID OF DISHONOUR

This and other titles by Heidi Rice are available in eBook format from www.millsandboon.co.uk

To all those people who asked me
when I was going to write Ella's story.

Now you know.

I hope it lives up to expectations! x

CHAPTER ONE

NEXT TIME YOU BOOK a holiday of a lifetime, don't choose the world's most popular couples' destination, you muppet.

Ella Radley adjusted her backpack and flinched as it nudged the raw skin that still stung despite spending yesterday hiding out in her deluxe ocean-view room at the Paradiso Cove Resort in Bermuda—AKA Canoodle Central.

Ella sighed—nothing like getting third-degree sunburn in the one place you couldn't reach to remind you of your single status. Not that she needed reminding. She stared in dismay at the line of six couples, all in various stages of loved-up togetherness, on the dock ahead of her as she waited to board the motor cruiser at the Royal Naval Dockyards on Ireland Island for what the dive company's website had promised would be 'a two-hour snorkel tour of a lifetime'. Unfortunately, she'd booked the tour when she'd first arrived nearly a week ago, before she'd been hit on by a succession of married men and pimply pubescent boys, napalmed all the skin between her shoulder blades and generally lost the will to have anything remotely resembling a lifetime experience.

Her best friend Ruby had once told her she was far too sweet and eager and romantic for her own good. Well, she was so over that. Frankly, paradise and all its charms could get lost. She'd much rather be icing cupcakes in Touch of Frosting's cosy café kitchen in north London—and laughing about what a nightmare her dream holiday had turned out to be with her business partner and BFF Ruby—than standing in line to take a snorkelling tour of a lifetime that would probably give her a terminal case of seasickness.

Stop being such a grump.

Ella gazed out across the harbour, trying to locate at least a small measure of her usual sunny outlook on life. Yachts and motor boats—dwarfed by the enormous cruise ship anchored across the harbour—bobbed on water so blue and sparkly it hurt her eyes. She recalled the pink sand beach they'd passed on the way in, framed by lush palms and luxury beach bungalows, which looked as if it had been ripped from the pages of a tourist brochure.

She only had one more day to fully appreciate the staggering beauty of this island paradise. Maybe booking this holiday hadn't been the smartest thing she'd ever done, but she'd needed a distraction... The trickle of panic crawled over her skin, making her aware of the familiar clutching sensation in her belly. She pressed her palm to the thin cotton of her sundress, until it went away again. She needed this day trip—to get her out of her room before the panic overwhelmed her or, worse, she became addicted to US daytime soaps.

The line moved forward as a tall man appeared at the gangplank wearing ragged cut-offs and a black T-shirt with the dive company's logo on it, his face shadowed by a peaked captain's cap. Ella stopped breathing, her eyes narrowing to minimise the glare off the water, astonished to discover that the steely-haired Captain Sonny Mangold, whose weathered face beamed out from the photo on the website, appeared to be in amazing physical shape for a guy pushing sixty. Talk about a silver fox. Not that she could see his hair from this distance.

Captain Sonny began to welcome each couple aboard, his gruff American accent floating towards her on the still, muggy air, and sending peculiar shivers up Ella's spine, even though she couldn't make out what he was saying. The couple ahead of her, looking affluent and young and very much in love, were the last to block her view. As the captain helped them both aboard Ella stepped forward, anticipation making her throat dry. She took in the staggeringly broad shoulders and long muscular legs encased in denim cut-offs as his head dipped to tick off the list on the clipboard in his hand. Wisps of dark blond hair clung to lean cheeks and a square, stubbled jaw, confusing her even more, then his head lifted.

All thoughts of nightmare holidays, canoodling couples and silver foxes blasted right out of her brain.

Goodness, he's stunning. And not much over thirty.

'You're not Captain Sonny,' she blurted, the wake-up call to her dormant libido blasting away her usual shyness too.

'Captain Cooper Delaney at your service.' The rich jade of his irises twinkled, and the tanned skin round the edges of his eyes creased. His arresting gaze dipped, to check the clipboard again. 'And you must be Miz Radley.' The laconic voice caressed her name, while his gaze paused momentarily on its journey back to her face, rendering the bikini she had on under her sundress half its normal size.

A large, bronzed hand, sprinkled with sun-bleached hair, reached out. 'Welcome aboard *The Jezebel*, Miz Radley. You travelling on your own today?'

'Yes.' She coughed, distressed as the answer came out on a high-pitched squeak. Heat flared across her scalp.

Good Lord, am I having a hot flush? Can he see it?

'Is that okay?' she asked. Then realised it sounded as if she was asking his permission.

'Sure.' His wide sensual lips lifted but stopped tantalisingly short of a grin—making her fairly positive he knew exactly how he was affecting her.

The blush promptly went radioactive.

'As long as you don't have any objections to me being your snorkel buddy?' He squeezed her fingers as she stepped aboard. 'We don't let clients dive alone. It's safer that way.'

The pads of her fingertips rubbed against the thick calluses on the ridge of his palm. And the tips of her already constricted breasts tightened.

'I don't have any objections,' she said, feeling stupidly bereft when he let go of her hand—and thinking that even on their ten-second acquaintance she'd hazard a guess that Captain Cooper Delaney was the opposite of safe. Why for the first time in a long time she should find that exhilarating instead of intimidating made her wonder exactly how stressed she'd been in the last week.

'How about you sit up front with me?'

It didn't sound like a question, but she nodded, her tongue now completely numb.

His palm settled on the small of her back, just beneath the line of her sunburn. He directed her past the other passengers as she struggled not to notice the hot tingles generated by his touch and the fresh scent of saltwater and soap that clung to him. Bypassing the single space left between the couples wedged onto the benches that rimmed the hull, he escorted her to one of the two seats in front of the console in the boat's cabin.

'There you go, Miz Radley.' He tipped his cap, the gesture more amused than polite thanks to that tempting twinkle, then turned to address the other passengers.

She listened to him introduce himself and the two wiry teenage boys who were his crew for the day, then launch into a relaxed spiel about the twenty-five-minute voyage to the snorkel site called Western Blue Cut, the history of the sunken wreck they'd be exploring, the ecology of the reef and a string of safety tips. But all she really heard was the deliciously rusty texture of his voice while her mind wrestled with the question of exactly what being someone's snorkel buddy might entail.

It couldn't possibly be as intimate as it sounded. Could it?

But when he climbed into the seat beside her, his hand closed over the rounded head of the gear stick on the console and she swallowed past a constriction in her throat that felt a lot like excitement.

He adjusted the stick down, tapped a dial, pressed a button and the boat roared to life. She grabbed the rail at the edge of the console to stop from tumbling onto her butt. He slanted her an amused look as she scrambled back into her seat. Then hid his mischievous gaze behind a pair of sunglasses.

All the blood pumped back into her cheeks—not to mention the hot spot between her legs—as the motor launch kicked away from the dock, edged past the other boats in the marina, and left the walled harbour to skim over the swell towards the reef.

He flashed her an easy smile—that seemed to share a wicked secret. 'Hold on tight, miz. I'd hate to lose my snorkel buddy before we get there.'

The answering grin that flittered over Ella's lips felt like her first genuine smile in months—filling up a small part of the gaping hole that had opened up in the pit of her stomach over a week ago.

Maybe going on a holiday of a lifetime solo didn't completely suck after all.

'Well, honey, you've certainly captured Coop's attention.'

Ella's cheeks burned at the comment from the plump middle-aged woman in bright pink Bermuda shorts and an 'I Found My Heart in Horseshoe Bay' T-shirt who joined her at the rail as the boat bobbed on the reef.

They'd reached their destination ten minutes ago and were waiting for Captain Delaney and his crew to finish allocating the snorkelling equipment before they dived in.

Ella had to be grateful for the respite, because sitting in such close proximity to the man for twenty minutes had caused her usually sedentary hormones to get sort of hyperactive.

'Do you know Captain Delaney?' she asked, hoping to deflect the conversation while studiously ignoring the blip in her heartbeat.

After careful consideration, she'd figured out that Captain Delaney's attention had nothing to do with her and everything to do with his job. She was the only single passenger on the boat, and he was just being conscientious, ensuring she got her money's worth and enjoyed the trip. They hadn't been able to talk much on the ride out because of the engine noise, thankfully. Those sexy—and she was sure entirely impersonal—smiles he kept flashing at her were more than enough to tie her tongue in knots. A reaction that had propelled her back in time to the excruciating crushes of her teens when she'd always been rendered speechless in the presence of good-looking boys.

This was precisely why she preferred guys who were homely and safe rather than dangerous and super-hot. Being struck dumb on a date could get old really fast.

'We've known Coop for nearly a decade,' the woman said in her friendly mid-western drawl. 'Bill and I been coming back to St George every year since our honeymoon in ninety-two. And we never miss *The Jezebel*'s snorkel tour. Coop used to work as a deck hand for Sonny as a kid, got his captain's stripes a while back. Now he just pitches in from time to time.' The woman offered a hand. 'Name's May Preston.'

'Ella Radley, nice to meet you.' Ella shook the woman's hand, comforted by her open face, and easy manner—and intrigued despite herself by the unsolicited insight into the hot captain's past.

She recognised May from the resort. May and her husband Bill, whom she liked too, because he was one of the few married men at Paradiso Cove who didn't have a roving eye.

'You're a cute little thing, aren't you? And with that lovely accent.' May tilted her head, assessing Ella in that direct and personal way that only American tourists seemed able to do without appearing rude. 'I must say, I've always wondered what Coop's type was. But you're quite a surprise.'

The blush headed towards Ella's hairline. 'I wouldn't say I'm his type.' Perish the thought; her heart would probably stop beating if she believed that. She might find him extremely attractive, but dangerous men had never been good for her mental health. 'It's just that I'm a woman on my own and he's being polite and doing a good job.'

May let out a hearty chuckle. 'Don't you believe it, honey. Coop's not the polite type. And he usually spends his time peeling the single female clients off him, not offering them a personal service.'

'I'm sure you're wrong about that.' Far from stopping, Ella's heartbeat hit warp speed—stunned disbelief edging out her embarrassment.

'Maybe, maybe not.' May's smile took on a saucy tilt, which was about as far from doubtful as it was possible to get. 'But this is the first I've ever heard of the snorkel-buddy safety rule. And that's after twenty years of coming on this tour.'

Ella bided her time while wrestling with May's shocking comment, until the captain and his two deckhands had seen off all the other snorkellers. While fitting fins and masks, giving instructions about how far to stray from the boat, demonstrating some basic hand signals, advising people on how long they had before they should head back, and how to identify the paddle wheel from the wreck of the sunken blockade runner they'd come to see, Cooper Delaney appeared to be the consummate professional. In fact, he seemed so relaxed and pragmatic while handling the other passengers, Ella convinced herself May had to be mistaken about the snorkel-buddy rule—and wondered if she should even question him about it. Wouldn't she sound impossibly vain, bordering on delusional, suggesting he'd offered to partner her for reasons other than her own safety?

But then he turned from the rail, took off his sunglasses and his slow, seductive smile had all the blood pumping back into her nether regions.

She fanned herself with her sunhat. Goodness, either she was suffering from sunstroke or that smile had some kind of secret thermal mechanism.

He crossed the deck towards her, his emerald gaze even brighter than the dazzling expanse of crystal blue water.

'So, Miz Radley, you want to strip down to your swimsuit and I'll get you fitted up, then we can head out?'

He leaned against the console, his large capable hand very close to her hip.

She sucked in a sharp breath as her lungs constricted, only to discover the fresh sweat darkening the front of his T-shirt made his salt and sandalwood scent even more intoxicating.

Courage, Ella, just make a general enquiry so you know for sure where you stand.

'Is that absolutely necessary?' she asked.

''Fraid so. The salt water's bound to ruin that pretty dress if you don't take it off. You didn't forget your swimsuit, did you?' His smile tipped into a grin.

'No, I meant us snorkelling together.' Her nipples shot

back to the full torpedo as his gaze drifted south. 'Is that necessary?'

One dark eyebrow lifted in puzzled enquiry, the smile still in place.

'It's just that May Preston said she'd never heard of that rule.' The words tripped over themselves to get out of her mouth before her tongue knotted again. 'You know, about it being necessary for people to snorkel in pairs for safety's sake…' She began to babble, her tongue overcompensating somewhat. 'I know it matters with scuba-diving. Even though I've never actually scuba-dived myself…' She cut off as his lips curved more.

Get to the point, Ella.

'I just…I wondered if you could confirm for me, why it's necessary for us to be snorkel buddies? If I'm only going to be a few yards from the boat?'

'Right.'

The word rumbled out and seemed to echo in her abdomen. He muttered something under his breath, then tugged off his captain's cap, revealing curls of thick sun-streaked hair damp with sweat flattened against his forehead.

'What I can confirm…' he slapped the cap against his thigh, the smile becoming more than a little sheepish '…is that May Preston's got one hell of a big mouth. Which I'm going to be having words with her about as soon as she gets back aboard this boat.'

'It's true?' Ella's eyes widened, her jaw going slack. 'You really did make it up? But why would you do that?'

Cooper Delaney watched the pretty English girl's baby blues grow even larger in her delicate, heart-shaped face—and began to wonder if he was being taken for a ride.

Shy and hot and totally lost, with that tempting overbite, and her lush but petite figure, Ella Radley had looked cute and sort of sad when he'd spotted her at the back of the boarding line an hour ago. Then her skin had flushed a ruddy pink as soon as he'd so much as smiled at her and she'd totally captivated him.

That nuclear blush had been so damn cute, in fact, that he'd been momentarily mesmerised and the snorkel-buddy rule had popped into his head and then spilled out of his mouth without his brain ever even considering intervening.

But seriously? Could any woman really be this clueless? Even if she did have eyes big enough to rival one of the heroines in the manga comic books he'd been addicted to in middle school? And her nipples peaked under her sundress every time he so much as glanced at her rack? And her cheeks seemed to be able to light up on cue?

No way. No one was that cute. It had to be an act.

But if it was an act, it was a damn good one. And he could respect that, because he'd dedicated his life to putting on one act or another.

Unfortunately, act or no, she'd caught him out but good.

Thanks a bunch, May.

He resigned himself to taking his punishment like a man, and hoped it didn't involve a slap in the face—or a sexual harassment suit.

'If I said because you looked like you could use the company,' he began, hoping that humour might soften the blow, 'would you buy it?'

The instant blush bloomed again—lighting up the sprinkle of freckles on her nose. 'Oh, yes, of course, I thought it might be something like that.' She shielded her eyes from the sun, tipping her chin up. 'That's very considerate of you, Captain Delaney. But I wouldn't want to put you out if you're busy. I'm sure I'll manage fine on my own.'

It was his turn for his eyes to widen at the earnest tone and the artless expression on her pixie face.

Damn, did she actually just buy that? Because if this was an act, it ought to be Oscar nominated.

No one had ever accused him of being considerate before. Not even his mom—and he'd worked harder at fooling her than anyone, because she'd been so fragile.

'The name's Coop,' he said, still not convinced that he'd got off the hook so easily, but willing to go with it. 'Believe me. I'd be happy to do it.' He tried to emulate her earnest expression. Although he figured it was a lost cause. He'd learnt at an early age to hide all his emotions behind a who-the-hell-cares smile, which meant he didn't have a heck of a lot of practice with earnest.

Her lips curved and her overbite disappeared. 'Okay, if you're absolutely sure it's not a bother.' The blue of her eyes brightened to dazzling. 'I accept.'

The smile struck him dumb for a moment, turning her expression from cute to super-hot but still managing to look entirely natural. Then she bounced up to pull her sundress over her head. And the punch of lust nearly knocked him sideways.

Bountiful curves in all the right places jiggled enticingly, covered by three pitifully tiny triangles of purple spandex that left not a lot to the imagination—and had that cheesy sixties tune his mom used to sing on her good days about a teeny-weeny polka dot bikini dancing through his head.

Damn but that rack was even hotter than her smile. Her nipples did that bullet-tipped thing again and he had to grit his teeth to stop one particular part of his anatomy from becoming the total opposite of teeny-weeny.

But then she turned, to drop her dress into the purse she had stowed under the dash, and he spotted the patch of sun-scorched flesh that spread out between slim shoulder blades and stretched all the way down to the line of her panties.

'Ouch, that's got to hurt,' he murmured. 'You need a

higher factor sun lotion. The rays can be brutal in Bermuda even in April.'

She whisked around, holding the dress up to cover her magnificent rack—and the nuclear blush returned with a vengeance. 'I have factor fifty, but unfortunately I couldn't reach that spot.'

He scrubbed his hand over the stubble on his chin, playing along by pretending to consider her predicament. 'Well, now, that sounds like a job for your snorkel buddy.'

A grateful smile lit up her face, and he almost felt bad for taking advantage of her...until he remembered this was all some saucy little act.

'That would be fabulous, if you don't mind?' She reached back into her tote and pulled out some lotion.

Presenting her back to him, she lifted the hair off her nape as he squeezed a generous amount of the stuff, which had the consistency of housepaint, between his palms, and contemplated how much he was going to enjoy spreading it all over her soft, supple, sun-warmed skin.

Well, hell... If he'd known the good-guy act came with these kind of benefits, he'd have given it a shot more often.

CHAPTER TWO

DO NOT PURR, under any circumstances.

Ella bit back a moan as Cooper Delaney's work-roughened hands massaged her shoulder blades. Callused fingers nudged under the knot of her bikini to spread the thick sun lotion up towards her hairline. Tingles ricocheted down her spine as his thumbs dug into the tight muscles of her neck, then edged downwards. She trapped her bottom lip under her teeth, determined to keep the husky groan lodged in her throat where it belonged.

'Okay, I'm heading into the red zone.' The husky voice brushed her nape as his magic touch disappeared and she heard the squirt of more lotion being dispensed. 'I'll be gentle as I can, but let me know if it's too much.'

I could never have too much of this.

She nodded, knowing any further attempt at speech would probably give away how close she was to entering a fugue state.

'Right, here goes.'

Light pressure hit the middle of her back as his palms flattened against the burnt patch. She shuddered, the sting nothing compared to the riot of tingles now rippling across her skin and tightening her nipples.

'You okay?' The pressure ceased, his palms barely touching her.

'Yes. Absolutely. Don't stop.' She shifted, pressing back into his palms. 'It feels…'

Glorious? Blissful? Awe-inspiring?

'Fine…' she managed, but then a low hum escaped as he began to massage more firmly. His thumbs angled into the hollows of her spine, blazing a trail of goosebumps in their wake.

She'd been far too long without the touch of a man's hands. That fabulous sensation of flesh on flesh, skin to skin. She stretched under the caress, like a cat desperate to be stroked, the tingles rippling down to her bottom as his thumbs nudged the edge of her bikini panties. She closed her eyes, willing the firm touch to delve beneath the elastic, while the hot heavy weight in her abdomen plunged.

Arousal zapped across her skin, and she had to swallow the sob as the exquisite, excruciating sensations pounded into her sex after what felt like decades on sabbatical.

Then disappeared.

'All done.'

Her eyes snapped open too fast, making her sway. His hand touched her hip, anchoring her in place—and snapping her back to reality.

'Steady there.' The amused tone had the blush firing up her neck.

Oh, no, had he heard that strangled sob? Could he tell she'd been hurtling towards a phantom orgasm?

Humiliation engulfed the need.

She was so going to unpack the vibrator Ruby had bought her for the trip, and test-drive it in her room tonight. Deciding she wasn't highly sexed enough to need artificial stimulation had obviously been way off the mark. And Ruby had once sworn by hers—before she'd found her husband, Callum.

'That should keep you from getting barbecued again, at any rate.' The rough comment intruded on her frantic debate about the merits of vibrators. And the blush went haywire.

She stretched her lips into what she hoped looked like a grateful smile—instead of the first stages of nymphomania. 'I really appreciate it.'

She watched as he snapped the cap onto the lotion bottle. Only to become momentarily transfixed by the sight of those long, blunt, capable fingers glistening in the sunlight from the oily residue.

'There you go.' He held out the lotion bottle as another inappropriate jolt of arousal pulsed into her sex.

Locating her backpack, she spent several additional seconds shoving the bottle back into it, pathetically grateful when her hands finally stopped trembling. Maybe if she drew this out long enough the blush might have retreated out of the forbidden zone too.

'Thank you, that was…' She groped for the right word—awesome being definitely the wrong word, even if it was the one sitting on the tip of her tongue.

'You're welcome.'

Her lungs seized at the glow of amusement in the deep green depths of his eyes. The blip of panic returned as she got lost in the rugged male beauty of his face—the chiselled cheekbones, the shadow of stubble on the strong line of his jaw, the tantalising dimple in his chin.

How could any man be this gorgeous? This potently male? It just wasn't fair on the female of the species.

The sensual lips twitched, as if he were valiantly suppressing a grin.

Get a flipping grip. The man offered to be your snorkel buddy, not your bonk buddy.

'So we're all set?' The rough question echoed in her sex.

'Unless you need me to return the favour?' She coughed, when the offer came out on an unladylike squeak. 'With the sun lotion, I mean. So you don't burn.'

The suggestion trailed off as his eyebrows lifted a fraction and the edge of his mouth kicked up in one of those sensual, secret smiles that had been making her breathing quicken all morning. It stopped altogether now.

Shut up. You did not just say that? You sad, sad, sex-deprived nymphomaniac.

'Forget it, that was a silly thing to say.' She raced to cover the gaff. 'I don't know why I suggested it.' Cooper Delaney's sun-kissed skin had the healthy glow of a year-round tan weathered by sea air. He'd probably never had to use lotion in his entire life. 'I'm sure you don't need to worry about sunburn. Perhaps we should just—'

'That sounds like a great idea.' The easy comment cut through her manic babble.

'It does?'

His lips kicked up another notch. 'Sure, you can never have enough protection, right?'

Was he mocking her? And could she summon the will to care while she was barely able to breathe?

'Um, right. I'll get the lotion, then.' She dived back into her bag, rummaging around for what felt like several decades as she tried to locate the lotion before he changed his mind. She found it just in time to see him lift the hem of his T-shirt over his head and throw it over the console.

All the blood rushed out of her brain as she stood, poised like the Statue of Liberty, clutching the lotion like Liberty's torch.

Oh. My. God. His chest is a work of art.

Sun-bleached hair curled around flat copper nipples as if to accentuate the mounds of his exceptionally well-defined pecs. She followed the trail down between the ridged muscles of his six-pack, then swallowed convulsively as the thin strip of hair tapered beneath the waistband of his cut-offs, drawing her attention to the roped sinews that stood out in bold relief against the line of his hip bones.

No wonder it's called a happy trail. I feel euphoric.

'Thanks, honey. I appreciate it.' His gruff words interrupted her reverie as he presented her with an equally breathtaking view of his back.

His spine bisected the slabs of packed muscle, sloping down to the tattoo of a Celtic Cross, inked across the base of his back, which peeked out above his shorts. Her gaze dipped lower, to absorb the sight of a perfectly toned male ass framed in battered denim.

She cleared her throat loudly, before she choked to death on her own drool. 'Is, um, is factor fifty okay?'

He lifted one muscular shoulder, let it drop. 'Whatever you've got is good.'

The low words seemed to rumble through her torso, making her pulse points vibrate.

She squeezed a lake of the viscous white liquid into unsteady palms. Taking a deep breath, she flattened her palms onto the hot, smooth skin of his back, while her lungs clogged with the tempting scent of cocoa butter and man.

The muscles tensed as she spread the thick lotion, and absorbed the heat of his skin, the steely strength beneath.

Moisture gathered in the secret spot between her thighs, which now felt as if it was swollen to twice its normal size.

As she spread the white liquid over the wide expanse of his back, and massaged it into his skin, she timed her breathing to the beat of the timpani drum in her ear, in a desperate attempt to stop herself from hyperventilating.

And passing out before the job was done.

Cooper touched Ella's arm, signalling with his index finger to draw her attention to the blue angel fish darting beneath the shelf of fiery orange coral. Her eyes popped wide behind the mask and her expressive mouth spread into a delighted grin around her mouthpiece.

As they hovered above the reef he watched her admire the brilliant aquamarine of the fish's scales, the white-tipped fins, and the pretty golden edging on the tail, while he admired the open excitement on her face and the buoyant breasts barely contained by purple spandex.

His groin twitched, the blood pumping south despite the chill of the seawater. The sudden flashback, of her stretching under his hands, her breathing coming out on a strangled groan as he caressed the firm skin, didn't do much to deter the growing erection.

He adjusted his junk, grateful for the wet denim of his shorts. Which had been holding him in check ever since he'd dived into the ocean, leaving Dwayne to fit Ella's flippers and snorkelling gear, before she spotted the telltale ridge in his pants.

They'd been out on the reef for over half an hour now, and he'd mostly got himself under control. But the sight of that shy, excited smile, every time he showed her some new species of fish, or the barnacled wreck of the *Montana*, had been almost as mesmerising as the feel of her fingers fluttering over his bicep whenever she wanted to point something out to him, or the sight of all those lush curves bobbing in the waves.

The woman was killing him. So much so that his golden rule about hooking up with single lady tourists was in danger of being blown right out of the water.

As she pointed delightedly to a shoal of parrot fish flicking past he recalled why he'd made his golden rule in the first place.

Single ladies on holiday generally fell into one of two categories: those on the hunt for no-strings thrills, or those on the look-out for an exotic island romance. As both scenarios invariably involved lots of sex, he'd been more than happy to indulge in hook-ups with the clients when he'd first arrived on the island a decade ago. But back then he'd been eighteen going on thirty with a chip on his shoulder the size of a forest, not a lot of money and even fewer prospects.

In the intervening years, he'd worked his butt off to leave that messed-up kid in the dust. As the owner of a lucrative and growing dive-shop franchise, he sure as hell didn't need to look for acceptance in casual sex any more—or the hassle of pretending to be interested in more.

Which meant single lady tourists had been off limits for a while, unless he knew for certain they weren't after more than the one night of fun. Usually, it was easy enough to figure that out. In fact he'd become an expert at deciding whether a woman had lust or stardust in their eyes when they hit on him. But Ella Radley didn't fit the profile for either.

For starters, she hadn't exactly hit on him despite the obvious chemistry between them. And he still hadn't figured out whether that enchanting mix of artless enthusiasm, sweet-natured kookiness and transparent hunger was all part of an act to get into his pants—or was actually real.

Unfortunately, he was fast running out of time to make up his mind on that score. Sonny had two more fully booked tours scheduled right after this one. And with the old guy's arthritis acting up again, Cooper had agreed to step in and captain them. It was a responsibility he couldn't and wouldn't duck out of. Because Sonny and he had a history.

The old guy had offered him a shift crewing on *The Jez*, when he'd been eighteen and had just spent his last dime on boat fare to the island. He'd been sleeping rough on the quayside and would have sold his soul for a burger and a side order of fries.

He'd done a half-assed job that afternoon, because he'd been weak from hunger and didn't know the first thing about boats. But for the first time since his mother's death, he'd felt safe and worth something. Sonny had given him hope, so whatever debt the old guy called in, he'd pay it.

All of which meant he had to make a decision about Ella Radley before they got back to the dockyards. Should he risk asking her out tonight without being sure about her?

She swam back towards him, her eyes glowing behind the mask, then made the sign for okay.

He gave her a thumbs up and then jerked it towards the boat. They'd run out of time ten minutes ago. Everyone else would be back on the launch by now ready to head back to the mainland. Which meant it was past time for him to make his mind up.

But as she swam ahead of him, her generous butt drawing his gaze with each kick of the flippers, heat flooded his groin again, and he knew his mind had already been made up... Because his brain had stopped making the decisions a good forty minutes ago, when those soft, trembling hands had stroked down his spine and hovered next to the curve of his ass. And he'd heard her sigh, above the rush of blood pounding in his ears.

Ella gripped the rail as the launch bumped against the dock and her snorkel buddy sent her one of his trademark smiles.

He laid his palm on her knee and gave it a squeeze, sending sensation shooting up her thigh. 'Hold up here, while I get everyone off the boat.' The husky, confidential tone had her heart beating into her throat, the way it had been doing most of the day.

She forced herself to breathe evenly, and take stock, while he and his crew docked the boat and he bid farewell to the rest of the passengers.

Do not get carried away. It's been an amazing morning, but now it's over.

The snorkel tour, the epic beauty of the reef and its sealife had totally lived up to the hype. But it had been Cooper Delaney's constant attention, his gorgeous body and flirtatious smile, that had turned the trip into a once-in-a-lifetime experience.

He'd made her feel special—and for that she couldn't thank him enough. Which meant not overreacting now and putting motivations into his actions that weren't there.

She gulped down the lump of gratitude as she watched him charm May Preston, and give her husband a hearty handshake. Once they'd gone, it would be her turn to say goodbye.

May waved, then winked—making the colour leech into Ella's cheeks—before handing a wad of bills to Cooper. He accepted the money with a quick lift of his cap.

A tip.

Shame tightened Ella's throat as Cooper folded the bills into the back pocket of the jeans he'd changed into. Of course, she should tip him. That would be the best way to thank Cooper for all his attention. And let him know what a great time she'd had.

She grabbed her backpack, found her purse, then had a minor panic attack over the appropriate amount. Was twenty dollars enough? Or thirty? No, forty. Forty, would work. After all, he'd surely need to share it out with the boys in his crew. She counted out the money, her palms sweating, hoping she'd got the amount right. She wanted to be generous, even though she knew that any amount couldn't really repay him for what he'd done.

For two amazing, exhilarating, enchanting hours she'd completely forgotten about all her troubles—and felt like a woman again, a whole, normal, fully functional woman—and for that no tip, however generous, could be big enough.

Slinging the pack over her shoulder, she approached him with the bills clutched in her fist. Now, how to hand it over without blushing like a beetroot?

He turned as she approached, that killer smile making her pulse hammer her neck. The appreciative light in his eyes as his gaze roamed over her had her bikini top shrinking again.

'Hey, there.' The killer smile became deadly. 'I thought I told you to stay put.'

She pursed her lips to still the silly tremble, unable to return the smile. 'I should get out of your way.'

'You're not in my way.' He tucked the curl of hair that had escaped her ponytail back behind her ear—in a casually possessive gesture that only made the tremble intensify. 'But I've got a couple more tours to run today. How about we meet up later? I'll be at a bar on the south side of Half-Moon Cove from around seven onwards…'

Blood thundered in her ears, so she could barely make out what he was saying.

'What d'you say?' he continued. 'You want to hang out some more?'

She nodded, but then his knuckle stroked down her cheek.

Panicked by the clutch of emotion, and the insistent throb of arousal, she shifted away from his touch. Time to make a quick getaway, before the lip quiver got any worse.

She thrust the bills towards him. 'I've had an incredible time. The tour was amazing. Thank you so much.'

His gaze dropped. 'What's this?'

'Umm, I hope it's enough.' Had she miscalculated? Was it too little? 'I wanted to thank you properly, for all the trouble you went to this morning.'

A muscle in his jaw hardened. And she had the strangest feeling she'd insulted him. But then he blinked and the flash of temper disappeared.

'Right.' He took the bills, counted them. 'Forty dollars. That's real generous.' She thought she detected the sour hint of sarcasm, but was sure she must be mistaken when he tipped his cap and shoved the bills into his back pocket.

'Thanks.' For the first time, the easy grin looked like an effort. 'I'll see you around, Miz Radley.'

The clutching feeling collapsed in her chest, at the formal address, the remote tone.

Had she just imagined the invitation for later in the evening? Or, worse, blown it out of all proportion? Obviously it had been completely casual and she'd made too much of it.

She stood like a dummy, not knowing what to do about the sudden yearning to see the focused heat one more time.

The moment stretched out unbearably as he studied her, his expression remote and unreadable.

'I suppose I should make a move,' she managed to get out at last.

Get off the boat. He probably has a ton of things he needs to be doing.

'Well, thank you again.' *You've said that already.* 'It's been so nice meeting you.' *Stop gushing, you nitwit.* 'Goodbye.' She lifted her hand in a pointless wave that immediately felt like too much.

'Yeah, sure.' He didn't wave back, the words curt, his face blanker than ever.

She rushed down the gangplank, refusing to look back and make an even bigger ninny of herself.

CHAPTER THREE

ELLA HELD THE plastic column, flipped the switch. Then yelped and dropped it when it shivered to life with a sibilant hum. She signed and flicked the switch back down to dump the vibrator back in its box.

Damn, trying out the sex toy had seemed like such a good idea when she'd been with Cooper, while all her hormones were jumping and jigging under his smouldering stare.

But after their awkward parting, she wasn't feeling all that enthusiastic about discovering the joys of artificial stimulation any more.

Plastic just didn't have the allure of a flesh and blood man. Plus the way things had ended had flatlined all the jiggling. She just felt empty now, and a little foolish, for enjoying his company so much when it hadn't meant anything. She racked her brains to figure out what had happened. Because one minute he'd been laid-back and charming, oozing sex appeal, and asking her if she wanted to 'hang out' later and the next he'd been cold and tense and dismissive.

The phone rang, jolting her out of her dismay. She groped for the handset, grateful for the distraction, especially when her best friend's voice greeted her.

'Ella, hi, how's things in paradise?'

Ella smiled, happiness at the sound of Ruby's voice tempered with a surge of homesickness. 'Ruby, I'm so glad you called.' She gripped the phone, suddenly wishing she could levitate down the phoneline.

Other than this morning's snorkelling trip of a lifetime with the gorgeous—and confusing—Captain Cooper, her trip to Bermuda had been a disaster. She wanted to go home now.

'Is everything okay? You sound a little wobbly.'

'No, everything's good. I guess I'm just over paradise now.'

Ruby laughed, that rich, throaty, naughty laugh that Ella missed so much. 'Uh-oh, so I'm assuming you still haven't met any buff guys in Bermuda shorts, then?'

'Umm, well.' The image of Cooper's exceptionally fit body, his low-slung cut-offs clinging to muscular thighs, that mouth-watering chest gilded with seawater, and the devastating heat in his eyes, popped into Ella's head and rendered her speechless.

'You have met someone, haven't you?' Ruby said, her usual telepathy not dimmed by thousands of miles of ocean. 'Fantastic! Auntie Ruby needs to know all the details.'

'It's nothing, really. He's just a cute guy who was captaining the snorkel tour I went on this morning. We flirted a bit.' At least, she thought they'd been flirting, but maybe she'd got that wrong too. 'But he's not my type at all. He's far too sexy.' She recalled his callused hands, massaging the thick suncream into her skin—and wondered if Ruby could sense her hot flush from the UK.

Ruby snorted. 'Are you on crack or something? There's no such thing as too sexy. Ever. And clarify "a bit"—does that mean there might be an option for more?'

'Well, he did sort of ask me out.'

'That's fantastic.'

'But I don't think I'll follow it up.'

Her mind snagged on their awkward parting. As flattering as Cooper's undivided attention had been, and as exciting as she'd found snorkelling with him—cocooned together in the exhilarating cool of the ocean as he used sign language to point out the different colourful fish, the sunken wreck of an old schooner and the majestic coral—it hadn't ended all that well.

She pictured again the tight line of his jaw when she'd handed him the hefty tip, and winced at the memory of his curt goodbye.

'Why not?' Ruby asked. 'I thought that was the whole point of this holiday. To have a wild, inappropriate fling and kick-start your sex life?'

'What?' Ella could feel the blush lighting her face like a Christmas tree. 'Who told you that?'

'You did. You said you needed to get away, and rethink your priorities. That you'd become too fixated on finding the right guy, when what you really needed was to find a guy,' Ruby replied, quoting words back to Ella she couldn't remember saying.

She'd been in a fog at the time, probably even in a state of mild shock after visiting her local doctor. She'd booked the holiday at the last minute, packed and headed for the airport the very next day, partly because she hadn't known how to tell Ruby her news. For the first time ever, she'd been unable to confide in her best friend, and that had been the scariest thing of all.

'I thought that's what you meant,' Ruby finished, sounding thoroughly confused now. 'That you were heading to Bermuda to get laid.'

'Not precisely.' Ella felt the weariness of keeping the secret start to overwhelm her.

'So what did you mean?' Ruby's sharp mind lasered straight to the truth. 'This has something to do with the doctor's appointment you had the day before you left, doesn't it? I knew something had freaked you out. What aren't you telling me?'

Ella could hear the urgency in Ruby's voice and knew her friend's natural tendency to create drama was about to conjure up a terminal illness.

'Whatever it is, you have to tell me, Ell. We can sort it out. Together. We always have.'

'Don't worry, Rube.' Ella began talking her friend down from the ledge. 'It's nothing terrible.' Or not that terrible.

'But it does have something to do with the appointment?'

'Yes.'

'Which is?' Ruby's voice had taken on the stern fear-of-God tone she used with her three children, which instantly made them confess to any and all infractions.

Ella knew she wouldn't last two seconds under that kind of interrogation. Even from four thousand miles away. 'Dr Patel took some tests. I'll get the results on Monday.' She blew out a breath, the hollow pressure that had dragged down her stomach a week ago feeling as if it had become a black hole. 'But given my mum's history and the fact that I haven't had a period now in over three months, she thinks I might be going into premature menopause.'

'Okay,' Ruby said carefully. 'But it's just a possibility? Nothing's certain yet?'

Ella shook her head, the black hole starting to choke her. 'I'm pretty certain.'

She'd done something cowardly in her teens, that she'd always believed she would be punished for one day. And sitting in Myra Patel's office, listening to her GP discuss the possible diagnoses, the prospect of a premature menopause had been both devastating, and yet somehow hideously fitting.

She placed her hand on her abdomen to try and contain the hollowness in her womb, and stop it seeping out and invading her whole body. 'I've left it too late, Ruby. I'm not going to be able to have children.'

'You don't know any such thing. Not until you get the tests back. And even if it is premature menopause, a couple of missed periods isn't suddenly going to make you infertile.'

She did know, she'd known ever since she was eighteen and she'd come round from the anaesthesia in the clinic to find Randall gone. She didn't deserve to be a mother, because the one time she'd had the chance she'd given it up to please a guy who hadn't given a hoot about her.

'I suppose you're right,' she said, humouring Ruby.

'Of course I am. You're not allowed to go the full drama until you get the results. Is that understood?'

'Right.' Her lips wrinkled, as she found some small measure of humour in having Ruby be the one to talk her off the ledge for a change.

'Now.' Ruby gave an exasperated sigh. 'I want to know why you didn't tell me about this? Instead of giving me all that cryptic nonsense about finding a guy to shag.'

'I never said shag.' Or at least she was fairly sure she hadn't.

'Don't change the subject. Why didn't you tell me about this before? Instead of running off to Bermuda?'

It was a valid question, because they'd always shared everything—secret crushes, first kisses, how best to fake an orgasm, even the disastrous end to her college romance with Randall, and Ruby's rocky road to romance with the sexy barrister who'd rear-ended her car on a Camden street seven years ago and turned out to be her one true love. But Ella still didn't know how to answer it.

'I just couldn't.' Her voice broke, and a tear escaped. One of the ones she'd been holding captive for over a week.

'Why couldn't you?' Ruby probed, refusing to let it go.

'I guess I was feeling shocked and panicky and inad-

equate...' She sucked in a breath, forcing herself to face
the truth. 'And horribly jealous. Of the fact that you have
such a wonderful family and three beautiful children and
I may never have any.' She let the breath out. There, she'd
said it. 'I felt so ashamed to be envious of you. Because
everything you have with Cal and the kids, you've worked
for and you deserve.'

The self-pitying tears were flowing freely now. She
brushed them away with the heel of her hand. Hoping Ruby
couldn't hear the hiccoughs in her breathing. 'I couldn't
bear for this to come between us in any way.'

'That's the most ridiculous thing I've ever heard.'

'Why?' The question came out on a tortured sob.

'Well, for starters, you don't want Cal. He's far too
uptight and bossy for you. His insistence on being right
about everything would make you lose the will to live
within a week.'

'Cal's not uptight and bossy. He's lovely.' Ella jumped
in to defend Ruby's husband, whom she adored, if only
in a purely platonic sense—because he actually was a little bossy.

'Only because he's got me to unwind him on a regular
basis, and boss him about back,' Ruby replied. 'But more
to the point.' Her voice sobered, the jokey tone gone. 'You
don't want my kids, you want your own. And if I deserve
my little treasures—not that Ally and Max were particularly treasurable this morning when they decided to de-
clare World War Three on each other using their Weetabix
as nuclear warheads—then you certainly do.'

Do I?

The question echoed in her head, but she didn't voice
it, Ruby's passionate defence counteracting at least some
of the guilt that had been haunting her for over a week.

'You're going to make an incredible mum one day,'

Ruby added with complete conviction. 'And, if you have to, there are lots of possible ways of achieving that.'

'How do you mean?'

'You know, like artificial insemination, IVF, donor eggs, surrogacy, adoption, that sort of thing.'

Ruby's matter-of-fact response shrank a little of the black hole in her belly. She hadn't considered any of those options yet, the prospect of infertility too shocking to get past. But why shouldn't she? If the worst came to the worst and Myra's diagnosis was correct?

'I guess you're right, I hadn't really—'

'But frankly,' Ruby interrupted, 'I think we're getting the cart before the stallion here.'

'Excuse me?'

'Ella, your biggest problem when it comes to having a child of your own is not the possibility of a premature menopause. It's the fact that every guy you've been out with since that tosser in college has been so mind-numbingly dull even I couldn't be bothered to flirt with them.'

Ella frowned, picturing the handful of guys she'd dated in the last decade. And realised that Ruby's outrageous statement might not actually be all that far off the mark— because she couldn't recall a single one of them with any degree of clarity.

When had dating become such an effort? And sex such a chore?

Was that why she'd had a rush of blood to the head at Cooper's casual suggestion of a drink later? Flirting with him had been exciting, exhilarating, and yet she'd totally freaked out when he'd offered her the chance to take it further.

What was that about? She was thirty-four, for goodness' sake, not ninety.

'The thing is, Ella,' Ruby continued, 'I know sexual

chemistry isn't everything in a relationship—and Randall the dickhead is a case in point.'

Ella winced at hearing Randall's name spoken aloud— a name they'd both avoided speaking for sixteen years. But the gaping wound her college boyfriend had caused— which she'd believed then would fester for the rest of her life—had scabbed over in the years since. Because the mention of his name didn't hurt any more; it only made her feel ashamed, that she'd fallen for him so easily, mistaken a couple of really spectacular orgasms for love, and then let him bulldoze her into doing something she would later regret.

'But sometimes chemistry can come in very handy, if you need a serious pick–me-up in the dating department,' Ruby continued. 'Which brings us right back to Captain Studly from your snorkel tour.'

Didn't it just?

'So tell me again,' Ruby continued. 'Why exactly can't you take him up on his offer of a date?'

'Because I'm not entirely sure he meant it.'

'And why would you think that? Talk me through it.'

'Well, he asked me if I'd like to hook up for a drink at this local hang-out after he finished work at seven and I panicked.' She'd chickened out, because Cooper Delaney had been more man than she'd had the guts to handle in a very long time—it all seemed so obvious now. 'And then I had to get off the boat, because he was busy. But it was all very casual, and we never agreed on anything specific.'

Even if the memory of Cooper's offer of a date thrilled her now, instead of terrifying her, the memory of his face, closed off and impassive, when she'd said that final goodbye wasn't far behind.

'Did this local hang-out have a name?' Ruby probed.

'No, but I think…' She searched her memory; hadn't he told her where it was? 'Half-Moon Cove.' The location echoed in her head in his deep American accent. 'He mentioned it was on the south side of Half-Moon Cove.'

'Fantastic. That's all we need.'

'It is?'

'Yes, now shut up and listen to Auntie Ruby.' Ruby paused, and the tickle of excitement in Ella's belly began to buzz as if she were being stroked by the vibrator. 'Captain Studly most definitely did invite you on a date. Time and location are all the specifics you need. And you are flipping well going to go on it.'

'But what if—?'

'No buts.' Ruby cut her off. 'It's way past time Ella Radley started dating the sort of man candy that might actually have some hope of exciting her enough to get her past first base.'

'I've been past first base in the past decade,' she said, indignantly—even if she couldn't remember the events in any great detail. 'But I don't think—'

'Uh-uh-uh, didn't you hear the "no buts" stipulation?' Ruby paused, but not long enough for Ella to form a suitable response. 'That goes hand in hand with the "no panicking" initiative. If you feel yourself starting to hyperventilate because Captain Studly is too Studly, just think of him as a test run. You need to get your flirt on, Ella, and he sounds like the perfect guy to practise on.'

And just like that, the buzz in Ella's belly sank even lower and became a definite hum.

CHAPTER FOUR

'YOU SURE YOU'RE okay here, ma'am? The Rum Runner isn't much for the tourists, just a local hang-out. I could take you to some nice places in Hamilton, where the cruise ships dock, no extra charge?'

'No, thank you, this is perfect, Earl.' Exhilaration fluttered in Ella's chest as she stepped out of the cab and surveyed the ramshackle bar at the end of the rutted beach road.

The twinkle of fairy lights on weathered wood added enchantment to the haphazard structure, which stood drunkenly, mounted on stilts over the water, as if it had downed one too many rum punches. The scent of the sea freshened the cloud of smoke and sweat as the customers spilled out of the saloon-style doors. The densely packed crowd smoked and chatted on the porch, while she could see couples dancing inside past the tables, swinging and swaying to the infectious soca beat, making the boardwalk pound beneath her sandals.

'You're sure this is the only place on the south side of Half-Moon Cove?' She handed Earl, her taxi driver, his fare and a generous tip through the cab window.

'Uh-huh.' Unlike Cooper, he sent her a wide smile as he tucked the money into the top pocket of his Hawaiian shirt. 'Cove's yonder.' He nodded towards a wide beach that began past the rocks at the end of the country road.

Edged by palm trees and vines and curving round the headland into the darkness, the cove lived up to its name, looking impossibly romantic as moonlight shimmered off the gently lapping surf.

'Ain't no other bars down here that I know of.' Pulling a card out of his pocket, he handed it to her. 'You give Earl a call when you need to get back. Not much traffic this way.'

After waving him off and watching the cab lights bounce out of sight down the unpaved road, she slipped the card into her bag, and slung the strap over her shoulder. Then she sucked in a fortifying breath and let it out in a rush.

Whether or not Cooper was here, she intended to enjoy herself. Ruby had given her the pep talk to end all pep talks, back at the hotel.

It was way past time she started living again, took the power back and charted her own course when it came to choosing the men she dated. And stopped boring herself to death with safe and secure and invited a little danger in. Bermuda with its colourful, chaotic nightlife and studly boat captains had to be the perfect place to start. Not least because if tonight went tits up, this particular dating disaster wouldn't be able to follow her home.

Ruby's words of dating wisdom had bolstered her courage as she'd showered, and waxed, and moisturised, and primped and perfumed. After far too much debate, she'd picked out an understated ensemble of skinny pedal-pusher jeans, heeled sandals and a lace-edged camisole. She'd pinned up her unruly hair, and plastered on a lot more make-up than she usually wore—as per Ruby's specific instructions—then dug out her favourite waterfall earrings and the cascade of cheap but cheerful bracelets she'd bought at Camden Market two weeks ago to complete the outfit.

The simple ritual of getting ready had helped temper her terror with a heady cocktail of excitement and anticipation.

Edging past the people milling around on the porch, she made her way to the bar. She'd have a couple of drinks and then, if Cooper didn't show, she could always ring Earl back and call it a night. At least she would have got to see something of the island before leaving.

The Rum Runner had a funky, relaxed vibe that reminded her of Sol's Salsa Joint on Camden Lock where Ruby and she and their wide circle of friends had once congregated on a Friday night to kick back after the working week. Ruby didn't go out much any more because of the kids, and most of their other friends had settled down and/or moved away in the last few years, so she'd slowly stopped going to Sol's too, but she'd always loved to dance and it occurred to her she'd missed the weekly ritual.

Her hips swung in time to the blast of horns and the fast infectious drum beat as the band on the stage in the far corner went into another number. She grinned as she wound her way through the packed tables—the soca rhythm an irresistible blend of joy and seduction—and felt the optimism that had always been so much a part of her personality seep back into her soul.

Slipping past a group of loudly dressed guys at the bar, she smiled back when one of them touched his beer bottle to his forehead in a silent salute.

'What'll it be, miz?' a barman addressed her once she had managed to inch past the crush of people and found a spot to rest her elbows on the bar. The thin layer of sweat on his dark skin made the red ink of the snake tattoo on his bicep glisten.

She tapped her toe to the bass guitar riff while checking out the names of the drinks scrawled on the chalkboard behind him—only a few of which she recognised. 'What would you recommend?'

'For you?' The lilting Caribbean accent matched the friendly twinkle in the barman's *café-au-lait*-coloured eyes. 'Only a Rum Swizzle will do.'

'That sounds wonderful.' She had absolutely no clue what that was. But tonight Ella Radley was on a mission, to get her flirt on and set it free. And for that, a Rum Swizzle sounded like just the ticket.

He returned a few minutes later and presented her with a tall icy glass of tangerine-coloured liquid, garnished with a chunk of pineapple, a swirl of orange peel and a maraschino cherry. She took a sip and the potent flavour of rum, fruit juice and liquor zinged off her tastebuds. So that was why they called it a Swizzle.

'Delicious,' she shouted over the music. 'How much do I owe you?'

'Not a thing.' A gold tooth winked in the pearly white of his smile. 'Your first Rum Swizzle in my place is always on the house.'

'You own this bar?'

He nodded. 'Sure do.'

A shot of adrenaline rushed through her to add to the hit from the rum. And Ruby's voice seemed to whisper in her ear.

Above all be bold—and seize the initiative—flirting is much more fun if you own it.

'Do you know a guy called Cooper Delaney?'

'Coop? Sure I know Coop. What do you want him for?' He sounded a bit put out. 'That boy's nothing but trouble.'

That was what she was counting on, she thought, the adrenaline more intoxicating than the Swizzle. She took another fortifying sip of the delicious concoction. 'Is he likely to be in tonight, do you think?'

She heard the eagerness in her tone but didn't care if it made her sound tarty. Discovering her inner flirt would be so much easier with a guy she already knew could make her hormones wake up and jiggle. And considering they'd been in hibernation, like, for ever, she needed all the help she could get.

The bartender's gaze was drawn to something past her shoulder. 'Yeah, he'll be in tonight.'

'Really, you're sure?' she said, then bit her lip.

Dial down on the tarty—that sounded a bit too eager.

'Uh-huh.' His dark gaze returned to her face.

'Back off, Henry. You're poaching.'

Ella spun round at the deep, wonderfully familiar accent—and the shot of adrenaline went into overdrive. Cooper Delaney had looked super-fit that morning in ragged denim, but he took fit to a whole new level in a dark blue polo shirt and black jeans. But then her head carried on spinning and she started to tilt.

A tanned hand shot out to grasp her upper arm and hold her upright. 'Damn it, Henry, how many of those things have you given her?'

'Only the one.' The barman, who Ella's slightly fuzzy brain had registered must be called Henry, sounded affronted.

'Oh, yeah?'

Ella blinked, hearing the edge in Cooper's usually relaxed tone. Was he mad about something? And what did it have to do with Henry, the benevolent barman?

Cooper slapped a couple of bills onto the bar with enough force to make her jump. 'That's for the rum punch, man. The lady's with me.'

Really? Fabulous.

So she hadn't imagined his offer of a date. The spurt of joy at the thought was quickly quashed, though, when his fingers tightened on her arm and he slanted her a look that didn't seem particularly pleased to see her. 'We're out of here.'

'But I haven't finished my drink.' She pivoted on her

heel, making a grab for her glass. But missed as he hauled her away from the bar.

'You've had enough.'

Henry shrugged and shouted after them, 'Sorry, miz. I told you he was no good.'

'You didn't have to pay for that,' she said, racing to keep up with his long strides as he marched past the tables and headed out into the night, dragging her along in his wake. 'Henry said it was on the house.'

'Yeah, I'll just bet he did.' Was that a snarl?

A succession of people called out a greeting to him or shouted across the crowd, but other than throwing back a quick wave of acknowledgement he barely broke stride. By the time they stepped off the deck and he swung her round to face him, she was breathless, the happy glow from her Swizzle fading fast.

'Okay, let's have it.' His shadowed face looked harsh in the half-light from the bar as he grasped both her arms, and made full use of his superior height. 'What are you doing here?'

'I…' And just like that her tongue swelled up, rendering her speechless. And all Ruby's advice about how to put her flirt on got washed away on a tidal wave of mortification.

He didn't look remote, the way he had when they'd parted that morning. He looked upset.

She'd made a terrible mistake—coming here when he hadn't really meant to…

'Because if you've come all the way out here to give me another smackdown, don't bother. I got the message the first time, sweetheart. Loud and clear.'

Smackdown? What smackdown?

'I should leave,' she blurted out, suddenly wishing that the worn floorboards of the bar's deck would crack open and swallow her whole. Or better yet whisk her back to her nice, quiet, ocean-view room at the resort.

Sticking to safe might be dull, but at least it didn't get you into these sorts of pickles. She'd never managed to piss off any of the guys she'd actually dated to this extent.

She sent a wistful glance back at The Rum Runner—the joyous dance music pumping out into the night. The lively bar had contained so many exciting possibilities less than five minutes ago. But as she stepped past him he didn't let go.

'Hey, hang on a minute.' The edge had left his voice. 'You didn't answer my question.'

'Was there a question in there?' she asked.

He didn't look mad any more, which she supposed was good.

But as his emerald gaze raked over her the focused attention made her breasts tighten. Humiliating her even more. Obviously her nipples were completely immune to his disapproval.

But then his wide lips quirked. 'It was never meant as a smackdown, was it?'

She tugged herself loose, and stepped back—starting to get annoyed. Okay, so she'd misinterpreted his offer of a date. Although how she had, she still wasn't sure. And her big coming-out party was officially a washout—but did he really have to gloat? And what was all this nonsense about a smackdown? 'I really have to go.'

She went to walk round him again. But his large hand wrapped around her wrist and drew her up short. 'Hey, don't... Don't go.'

He stood so close, the delicious scent of seawater and soap surrounded her. Making it a little hard for her to process the words. Was he apologising now? After all but biting her head off? 'Captain Delaney, I don't think—' she began.

'Call me Coop,' he murmured, the husky tone sending those tempting shivers of reaction back up her spine.

She drew in a breath, not able to recall a single one of Ruby's careful instructions as he stared down at her with the glint of appreciation in his eyes—and fairly sure she didn't want to any more. This evening had turned into a disaster.

She might as well face it, she would never be as good a flirt as Ruby, even if she took a degree course. She huffed out a breath. 'Listen, I genuinely thought you asked me here, and I had such a nice time this morning, I don't want to sour it now.' She hooked a thumb over her shoulder, feeling stupidly bereft at the thought of her party night ending so soon, and so ignominiously. 'But I really think I should go now.'

Because I'm a little concerned you might have a borderline personality disorder.

She came here to see you. You dumbass.

Warmth spread across Cooper's chest like a shot of hard liquor but was tempered by a harsh jolt of regret as he registered the wary caution in Ella's eyes—which looked even bigger accented with the glittery powder. Her lips pursed, glossy with lipstick in the half-light, as if she were determined to stop them trembling, crucifying him.

What the hell were you thinking? Behaving like such a jerk?

Even he wasn't sure what had gripped him when he'd walked into the bar and spotted her chatting with Henry, with that flushed excitement on her face. But the word that had echoed through his head had been unmistakable.

Mine.

And then everything had gone straight to hell.

Of course, his crazy reaction might have had something to do with the severe case of sexual frustration he'd been riding ever since she'd stepped aboard the boat that morning, but that hardly excused it. And the truth was he'd been handling it just fine, until the moment she'd handed him that wad of bills on the dock.

That was the precise moment he'd lost his grip on reality.

He'd been snarky and rude, acting as if she'd offered to kick him in the nuts, instead of giving him a forty-dollar tip.

He accepted tips all the time, to hand over to the kids who crewed the boat. Just the way Sonny had done for him when he was a kid.

He'd founded his business on the generosity of tourists like May Preston and her husband, who came back every year and always showed their appreciation way above the going rate. But when Ella had done the same, somehow he'd lost it. Instead of seeing her generosity and thoughtfulness for what it was, he'd been thrown back in time to the humiliation of his high-school days and the never-ending stream of dead-end jobs he'd taken on to keep him and his mom afloat. Back then, his teenage pride had taken a hit every time he had to accept a gratuity from people he knew talked trash about his mom behind his back. But he'd brushed that huge chip off his shoulder years ago, or at least he'd thought he had.

Why the weight of the damn thing had reappeared at that precise moment and soured his final few moments with Ella, he didn't have a clue, and he didn't plan to examine it too closely. All that mattered now was that he didn't blow his second chance with her.

That she'd come down to The Rum Runner at his suggestion was one hell of a balm to his over-touchy ego. The least he could do now was show her a good time. And given how cute and sexy she looked in those hip-hugger jeans and that skimpy tank it wasn't exactly going to be a hardship.

He raked his hand through his hair, trying to grab hold

of some of his usual charm with women, and think of how best to engineer his way back into her good graces after acting like such a douche.

Then he recalled how she'd been moving that lush butt while chatting to Henry, rocking her hips in time to the music. His pal Oggie's band played the opening sax solo, backed by the manic drum beat, of their best dance track. And he hoped he had his answer.

'You can't go back to the hotel. Not before you've danced to some real Bermuda soca with me.'

'I don't know...'

She glanced back at the bar, but he could hear her hesitation.

'Sure you do. It'll be fun.' He took her hand, lifted it to his lips and buzzed a quick kiss across her knuckles. 'You've come all this way. And I've acted like a jerk. So I owe you.'

'That's really not necessary.' She chewed on her bottom lip, the indecision in her voice crucifying him a little more.

'Sure it is. One dance. By way of an apology? That's all I'm asking.'

The shy smile was enough to tell him she'd forgiven him. But the sparkle of anticipation was tempered by caution. 'Okay, I don't see how one dance could hurt.'

'Awesome.' He placed his hand on her waist to direct her back into the bar, the spike of lust making his throat go dry when her hip bumped his thigh.

'It may be thirsty work, though,' she shouted above the bump and grind of drums and bass. 'Perhaps I should go back and get my Rum Swizzle?'

'Let's work up a sweat first,' he said, placing firm hands on her hips as he slotted them both into the packed dancefloor, the sweat already slick on his forehead. 'I'll buy you one later.'

Dancing with her was bound to be really thirsty work,

but he didn't plan to let her have any more Rum Swizzles.
Those damn things were lethal, especially on an empty
stomach—and with her tiny frame and that little stumble
at the bar after only half a glass, he would hazard a guess
Ella Radley was a really cheap drunk. He wanted her fully
conscious for the rest of the night, so he could enjoy her
company—and anything else she wanted to offer him.

Her perfume—a refreshing mix of citrus and spices—
drifted over him as she placed her hands lightly on his
shoulders and rolled her hips to the riotous bass beat in a
natural, unaffected rhythm that was more seductive than
original sin.

She grinned up at him, the cute smile a tempting mix
of innocence and provocation, then jerked up on her toes
to shout in his ear. 'Aye-aye, Captain. But be warned. I'm
on a mission tonight to get whatever I want.'

His hands tightened on her hips as her belly bumped
against him and his groin throbbed in time to the music.
'Not a problem, sweetheart.'

Because so am I.

'That's enough of that.' Coop lifted the sunshine drink
out of her hand and held it easily out of reach. 'I want you
able to walk out of here.'

Ella sent him a mock pout, but couldn't disguise her
happiness as his gaze settled on her face. The way it had
been doing all evening, with a gratifying combination of
possessiveness and desire.

They'd danced until they were breathless to the band's
medley of soca anthems, then eased into the seductive
moves of the soul tunes when they slowed the pace later
in the evening.

It was well after midnight now, and the bar had begun
to empty out. His large group of friends, most of whom
had come over to their table to banter with Coop or in-

troduce themselves to her, had mostly drifted away, leaving only a small group of die-hard couples on the dance floor still bumping and grinding with gusto and a scatter of people by the bar.

She'd danced with a few of the other guys, enjoying that relaxed, casual camaraderie that reminded her of her own friendship group back in Camden. But most of all she'd enjoyed the feel of Cooper's gaze on her throughout the evening—that said to everyone they were a couple. That— how had he put it?—she was with him, for the night. It had made her feel as if she belonged here, even though she was thousands of miles from home.

But more than that, his constant attention and that quick easy smile had both relaxed her and yet held a delicious tension, a promise of what was to come. Because she had no doubts whatsoever about where this was all headed. The smouldering looks, the proprietary touches, the irresistible scent of him, tangy and salty and spicy, wrapping around her in a potent blend of pheromones and sweat. And the delicious press of his erection outlined by the slow, seductive, sinuous moves of his muscular body as they danced.

The coil of desire had been pulsing in the pit of her stomach for hours now. Ready for him to make the next move—and if he didn't, she was ready to take the unprecedented step of making the move for him.

It was official. Ella Radley's flirt was now fully operational, the intoxicating buzz of the Rum Swizzles nothing compared to the glorious buzz of anticipation.

'And where exactly would I be walking to?' She arched an eyebrow, her tone rich with a confidence she'd thought had died inside her a lifetime ago.

His thumb brushed her cheek, his irises a mesmerising moss green in the bar's half-light. Resting his forehead on hers, he closed his fingers over her nape, that wandering thumb caressing the frantic pulse in her neck. 'My hut's down at the other end of the cove. You ready to take a stroll with me in the moonlight?'

It was the invitation she'd been waiting for, but the surge of excitement still made her giddy. She could already feel those rough, capable fingers on the slick flesh between her thighs. She wanted to taste him, touch him, inhale that delicious scent, and take the impressive ridge in his pants inside her. Her sex clasped and released, hollow and aching with the need to be filled.

Touching her lips to his, she licked across the seam of the wide, sensual mouth that had been driving her wild all day. The shot of adrenaline was as stimulating as the pulse of reaction when she heard him drag in a ragged breath. His fingers plunged into her hair, then clasped her head so his tongue could plunder.

She let him in, her tongue duelling with his as they sank into the ravenous kiss.

He broke away first, the pants of his breathing as thready as her own. 'I'm going to take that as a yes.'

She nodded, not sure she could speak around the joy closing off her throat.

Standing, he gripped her hand and hauled her out of her chair. He tossed a few dollars on the table, and sent Henry a parting salute. She waved her own goodbye at the barman, who was stacking glasses, a rueful smile on his face.

'See you around, pretty lady.' Henry waved back, shouting over the murmur of goodbyes being thrown their way by the bar's other remaining patrons. 'And don't you be doing anything I wouldn't, Coop.'

Coop dragged her outside, sending her a wicked grin over his shoulder as the night closed over them. 'Given what you would do, man,' he whispered for her ears alone, 'that gives me a hell of a lot of options.'

For some strange reason she found the comment riotously funny, her chuckle blending with the fading beat of music and the sound of the rolling and retreating tide as they stepped off the deck onto the beach. He laid his arm across her shoulders, tugged her into his side to lead her along the sand and into the darkness.

Crickets and night crawlers added an acoustic accompaniment to the flickering light of the fireflies in the undergrowth and the hushed lap of the water. She kicked off her sandals, picked them up, and let her toes seep into the damp sand.

The walk in the moonlight he'd promised went past in a blur, neither of them speaking, the only sound the sea, the insects and the rhythmic bump of her own heartbeat. A one-storey shack raised over the beach on a wraparound deck appeared as if by magic out of the undergrowth on the edge of the sand. A lamp suspended from the porch rail shone like a homing beacon, illuminating the rudimentary clapboard structure.

He dropped his arm from around her shoulders, to lace his fingers through hers and lead her up the steps onto the porch.

'You live here?' she asked, enchanted by the spartan dwelling.

'Yeah, mostly.' He held open the screen door to reveal a large, sparsely furnished, but tidy room. A sofa with well-worn cushions made up the living area, while a large mattress, the sheets neatly folded across the bottom, stood in front of the open deck. A tiny kitchenette cordoned off by a waist-high counter took up the hut's back wall, next to a door that she deduced must lead to a bathroom.

But it was the open deck, blending the hut's interior with the beach outside, that took her breath away. The silvery glow of the moon dipped over the horizon, shimmering over the water and making the dark sand look as if it disappeared into oblivion. The fresh scent of sea and salt and exotic blooms only added to the feeling of wild, untamed freedom that was so like Cooper himself.

'It suits you,' she said.

He huffed, the half-laugh both wry and amused. 'Why? Because it's cheap?' he said and she heard the cynical edge.

'No, because it's charming and unpretentious and unconventional.'

He turned up the lamp, giving the modest hut a golden glow.

Walking to the open deck, he closed two large shutters and then slid the screen door across, cocooning them in together against the Caribbean night. Only the sparkle of moonlight and the sound of surf and chirping insects seeped through the slats.

'Don't want to risk getting our butts bitten off by mosquitos,' he said, crossing the short distance back to her.

She laughed, the rough stubble on his jaw ticklish against her neck as he gripped her hips and nuzzled the sensitive skin beneath her ear.

'Especially such a cute butt,' he added, giving the butt in question an appreciative squeeze.

She wrapped her arms around his lean waist and slipped her fingers beneath the waistband of his jeans, to caress the tight muscles of the backside she had admired that morning in wet denim. 'I can totally get behind that sentiment.'

He chuckled, warm, callused palms sneaking under her camisole to glide up to her ribcage and send a series of tremors through her body.

'Flattery will get you everywhere,' he said. Before placing his mouth on hers at last.

Releasing his bum, she lifted arms lethargic with lust and draped them over his broad shoulders; driving her fingers into the soft curls at his nape, she let him devour her. He angled his hips and the thick ridge in his pants rubbed against her belly.

Oh, yes, I want this so much.

To be taken, to take. She wanted to let her body do the asking and have his answer, in the primordial mating ritual of two animals in need of an endorphin fix. The fact that she liked him, that he seemed a genuinely nice guy, didn't hurt. But right here, right now, as the building firestorm made the pulsing ache in her sex unbearable, and her nipples tighten into hard, swollen nubs, all she really cared about was satisfying the driving hunger.

His large hands rose from her waist to frame her face and she revelled in the primitive need making his eyes darken and the muscle in his jaw flex and release.

'Before we take this any further...' he trapped her against the hut's wall, the heavy ridge thickening even more '...I need to know if you're on the pill.'

Crushing disappointment cut through the fog of rum and arousal. 'You don't have any condoms? I don't either, I didn't think—'

'Hey, don't panic,' he interrupted. 'I've got condoms.'

'Oh, thank God.' Relief gushed like molten lava between her thighs.

'But I'm a belt and braces kind of guy. Condoms break.' He scooped her hair off her neck, pressed those clever lips to her collarbone, shattering her concentration. 'That's how I happened. I'm not looking to father another me.'

She heard the note of regret, and had the sudden urge to soothe. 'But you're so beautiful.' She cradled his lean cheeks between her palms, drew her thumb over one tawny brow and grinned into those piercing emerald eyes—which had crinkled at the corners with amusement. 'Your mother must have been so pleased to have you,' she said, loving the rasp of the manly stubble on his cheeks as all her inhibitions happily dissolved in the sweet buzz of Rum Swizzles and pheromones. 'Even if you were an accident.'

She heard his chuckle. Had she said something funny? She hadn't meant to.

'Not really.' He sent her the secret hey-there-gorgeous grin that he'd sent her when they were underwater and exploring the reef. Then it had flattered her, as if they were the only two people in the whole ocean allowed to explore its treasures; now it made her heart muscle squeeze and release, exciting her.

'Has anyone ever told you you're great for a guy's ego when you're hammered?'

'I'm not hammered,' she said, sure she wasn't. He'd only let her have two more Rum Swizzles, which he'd insisted on mixing himself behind the bar. And they hadn't tasted nearly as alcoholic as that first one. Plus she'd pigged out on the popcorn shrimp, some delicious jalapeño cheese things and the chips and dips and other nibbles that had appeared at their table as if by magic between dance sets. Right now she was pleasantly buzzed, but her senses felt heightened, more acute, not dull or fuzzy.

He touched his nose to hers. 'If you say so, miz,' he said in a perfect echo of Henry the friendly barman's Bermudan accent.

The spontaneous laugh turned to a staggered moan as his hands snuck under her camisole and cupped her breasts.

'Oh, yes.' She arched into the bold caress as his thumbs brushed her nipples, making the rigid peaks ache. 'That feels fabulous.'

He laughed. 'Stop distracting me and answer the damn question.'

She opened her mouth to ask what question, but then he plucked at one pulsating nipple, rolling it between his thumb and forefinger, and all that came out was a groaned, 'Yes.'

'Hallelujah.'

His teasing fingers left her breast to drag her top over

her head. And unclip the hook of her bra. He tugged his shirt over his head and tossed it over his shoulder, revealing the naked chest that she'd imagined touching all day.

Hallelujah indeed.

He boosted her into his arms, her back bumping the wall, as he wedged the hard ridge between her thighs, pressing it against the damp gusset of her jeans. She gripped his shoulders, her head spinning from the sensory overload. Then he ducked his head to capture one thrusting nipple between his lips and suckled hard.

Fire roared down to her core and she writhed, swivelling her hips to increase the pressure of his magnificent erection on that hot, sweet, swollen spot.

He blew across her wet breast, the cool air making it tingle and tighten more. 'Damn, but you're gorgeous.'

'So are you,' she said, admiring the bulge of his biceps as he held her up, the bunched pecs and sculpted abs, and the happy trail that bloomed into a forest of dark blond curls where his low-slung jeans had slipped down under the pressure of her clutching thighs.

'Can I see you naked? Please?' she asked.

His answering laugh sounded strained. 'I guess so, seeing as you asked so nice.' He dropped her suddenly, clutched her arm as she stumbled. 'Race you.'

She giggled as he hopped around on one foot, wrestling to get his boot off.

'Don't just stand there.' He tossed the boot across the room. 'Lose the damn pants or you'll have to pay a forfeit.'

Unbuttoning her jeans, she slipped them over her hips, going for the full stripper effect as she wiggled out of them, and loving the way his nostrils flared as he lost the other boot.

His wicked grin spread, and her heart rate accelerated, as he unhooked his trousers, shoved them down and kicked them off, not once taking his eyes off her.

Her gaze caught on the magnificent erection, standing proud in the nest of tawny curls. 'Wow...that's...really rather exceptional.'

He laughed. 'Have I told you, I love your accent?' He inclined his head towards the last piece of clothing she had on. 'Now lose the panties, before I rip them off.'

She whipped them off, twirled them on her finger and flung them away with a flourish.

'Good job.' He grabbed her wrist and dragged her to the bed, lying down beside her on the surprisingly comfy mattress.

She shivered, the light breeze coming through the shutters scented with the ocean.

His thumb trailed down her sternum. Then circled one heavy breast. She lifted up on her elbows to kiss him. The taste of the cola he'd been drinking all evening was as sweet as the weight of that exceptional erection cradled against her belly. Anticipation roared through her system. It had been so long since she'd felt this sexy, this aroused, this playful.

Ruby was right: why had she always been so serious about sex after college? She planned to correct that right now—she licked into his mouth, loving his staggered groan—with this gorgeous, hot, wonderfully reckless guy who was a gift she couldn't wait to unwrap.

His hands framed her face, his fingers plunging into her hair. She wrapped greedy fingers around the thick erection, slid her hand from root to tip, assessing its girth, its length, imagining it embedded into that aching, empty place between her legs.

But he swore softly as her thumb glided over the plump head, gathering the slick drop of moisture—and grabbed hold of her wrist, to tug her hand away.

'I'm way too close for that, sweetheart, but how about...?' His voice trailed off as he traced his thumb be-

tween her breasts, circled her belly button, then delved
into the hot, aching flesh of her sex.

Moisture flooded between her thighs.

She drew her knees up, let her head drop back, her sobs
of pleasure loud over the sound of surf and the rustle of
the breeze against their sweat-slicked bodies.

He circled and toyed with the slick nub, teasing the perfect spot. 'That's it, baby, I want to see you come for me.'

One large, blunt finger entered her, then another pushed
in beside it, stretching her, stroking the walls of her sex as
his thumb continued to play, to provoke. Sensation fired
across her skin, trapped her breath under her breastbone.
The coil of need tightened like a vice, the pleasure turning to devastating, delicious pain as it built to impossible
proportions but wouldn't let her go.

Clinging to his shoulders, urging him on, she pumped
her hips into his hand, riding that wonderfully devious
touch as she gave herself up to the riot of sensations.

Then he moved down on the bed, and disappeared between her knees. She shouted out in shock and delight as
his tongue lapped at her swollen clitoris. Then he captured
the slick nub between his lips and sucked. The coil yanked
tight and then exploded in a dazzling shower of sensation.
She sobbed—the long, thin cry of completion trapped in
her throat as his mouth drove her through the last magnificent swell of orgasm.

She pressed her legs together as he lifted his head, col-
lapsing back to earth. Shuddering and shaking, she opened
her eyes as he grinned down at her, his lips slick with her
juices.

The rumbled hum of his approval folded around her
heart like a caress.

'Sweeter than a Rum Swizzle,' he whispered, the sensual, playful grin even more beautiful than the rest of him.

The sight was so unbearably erotic, gratitude swelled in her chest, turning her voice into a throaty purr. 'Thank you.'

His lips tipped up at the edges. 'No need to thank me, baby, the pleasure was all mine.' He placed a kiss on the tip of her nose. 'But we're not finished yet,' he added, reaching across her to grab a foil packet from a glass jar on the upturned crate that doubled as a bedside table. He held it up. 'You want to do the honours, or should I?'

She lifted it out of his hand, her mouth watering at the thought of exploring that magnificent erection. And silently thanking him again for keeping things light and fun. 'Let me.'

She pushed his shoulder, until he lay on his back, that proud erection jutting up towards his belly button. Holding the packet in her hand, she licked the new bead of moisture off the tip. Savouring the taste of him. And eager to torment him the way he'd tormented her.

But the guttural groan was followed by a harsh expletive and before she could take him into her mouth he clasped her cheeks to hold her back.

'I'm sorry, sweetheart, but we're going to have to save that for later. I'm not Superman—and I don't want to disappoint you.'

He couldn't possibly disappoint her, she thought. But only laughed at his look of panic. 'Are you sure you're not Superman?'

'I used to be...' The confident smile returned as he rolled on top of her and snagged the condom packet out of her hand. 'But you're zapping all my super-powers.'

Ripping the foil with his teeth, he sheathed himself quickly, before nudging her thighs apart and settling between them. She felt the bulbous head nudge at her entrance as he held her hips, angling her pelvis.

She groaned as the thick shaft speared through the tight sheath, overwhelming her senses as her slick, swollen flesh stretched to receive him.

At last he was buried deep, pushing at her cervix. She gasped, astonished at the fullness, and how right, how exquisite it felt. She stroked his nape with unsteady fingers, enjoying the weight of him, the feeling of intimacy, and unity.

'I think you've boldly gone where no man has gone before.' She laughed, surprising herself with the ridiculous comment. But her heart felt so full, her body so magnificent, impaled on his. Could she come again? So soon after an orgasm? She certainly never had before, but with Cooper anything felt possible.

He swore, panting, the sinews of his neck straining beneath her fingers as he began to move. 'Damn it, woman, don't quote *Star Trek* at me now,' he grunted, between thrusts. 'Can't you see I'm trying to Klingon here.'

She snorted a laugh that choked into a sob as he stroked a place deep inside that triggered another unstoppable rush towards orgasm.

Goodness. I have a G-spot. Who knew?

'Touch yourself,' he demanded. 'I want you to come with me.'

She spread her own folds, blindly rubbing the stiff nub as he directed, feeling wild and untamed, greedily pursuing her own pleasure as the wave became sharper, sweeter, more glorious.

She rode the crest, his ragged grunts matching her loud moans, and soared towards oblivion with tears of joy and laughter—and staggered astonishment—hovering on her lids.

She drifted back to consciousness, the euphoria of afterglow slowly replaced by discomfort from the thick penis still lodged inside her.

He lifted off her, making her groan as her tight flesh struggled to release him.

'That was seriously awesome.' Flopping over onto his back, he lay with his arm over his face. 'You're incredibly tight.'

She felt herself blush, an odd combination of pleasure and acute embarrassment at the intimate comment. 'Only because you're so big,' she said, trying to find the playful tone again.

'While my ego and I thank you for that…' he dropped his arm to find her hand and thread his fingers through hers '…I'm not that much bigger than the average guy.'

The blush glowed. Maybe it wasn't just his size that had made him feel so large. Maybe it was because she hadn't done it with anyone in at least a year. And certainly never with that much energy or enthusiasm.

He turned onto his side, and cupped her cheek, his palm cool against her heated flesh. 'Has it been a while?'

She blinked, disconcerted by the perceptive comment. 'Are you a mind-reader?'

He touched her cheek, the tender, curious smile more seductive than the tangy scent of sex that surrounded them. 'How long?'

She huffed out a laugh, the embarrassment burned away by a new surge of arousal. 'Far too long, it seems.'

He hooked his thigh over her legs, shocking her when something stiff prodded her hip.

'Is that…?' She looked down, stunned to see him hard and ready again still sheathed by the condom.

He lifted her chin, grinning. 'Yeah, it is.' The cheeky grin—not to mention his astonishing powers of recuperation—made him seem very boyish. Too boyish.

'How old are you?' she asked, before she could think better of it.

His lips tilted. 'Nearly thirty.'

She propped herself up on her elbows. Good grief, he was still in his twenties. 'How nearly?'

'I'll be twenty-nine next month. Why? You planning to give me a present?' He cupped her breast, licked at the nipple. 'I can think of something I'd love to see gift-wrapped.'

'You're twenty-eight.' She scooted back. 'But that's… practically a toy boy.'

He chuckled, then grabbed her shoulders and shoved her onto her back, anchoring her in place with one hard thigh. 'Oh, yeah? So how old are you, then?'

'I'm thirty-four,' she said, indignantly.

His gaze drifted over her face. 'You don't look it.'

There didn't seem to be any judgment in the tone, but still she felt…embarrassed. 'Well, I am.' Maybe it was only six years but it felt like the wrong six years. 'Let me up.'

'Not going to happen, old lady,' he teased.

She struggled, trying to buck him off, but he didn't budge. 'Please, this feels awkward now.'

'Why? You're at your sexual peak. And so am I.'

Given the now-prominent feel of his erection, she had to agree. 'I know, but it feels weird.'

'It's not weird, it's cool.' He rubbed his shaft against her hip—making it fairly obvious he wasn't put off in the slightest by her vintage. She looked down at the thrusting erection. 'Although FYI, I'm not a toy boy,' he added. 'You're a damn cougar.'

A laugh popped out before she could stop it, but cut off when he cupped her sex. His fingers delved, stroking her oversensitive clitoris, the touch light and fleeting but enough to send shock waves of need echoing through her.

She thrust her fingers into his hair as he opened her thighs to position the impressive erection against her entrance. 'Well, I suppose, if you put it like—'

Grasping her hips, he thrust deep in one long, smooth,

all-consuming stroke, stealing her breath and cutting off any more pointless protests.

Oh, sod it.

Six years was nothing, she decided, especially once he'd established a slow, lazy, teasing rhythm that quickly became more intoxicating than the rum.

Hours later, Ella struggled to focus on the radiant glow of dawn peeping through the shutters. Contemplating the tenderness between her thighs and the soreness in other, previously unknown and now thoroughly exercised muscle groups, she conceded that, while the years might not be a problem, the mileage definitely was.

'I should go,' she mumbled, her fuzzy brain latching onto the fact that lingering past daybreak had the potential to be a lot more awkward than their age difference.

But when she lifted one tired limb, a muscular forearm banded round her midriff from behind and hauled her back into his embrace.

'Nothing doing,' Cooper's sleep-roughened voice murmured against her hair. His big body cocooned her, his chest solid against her back, the soft hairs on his thighs brushing the backs of her legs and the softening erection still prominent against her bottom.

She debated arguing with him, but couldn't fight the thundering beat of her pulse, the fatigue dragging her into oblivion or the novelty of being held so securely. Maybe she could stay and snuggle, for a little bit? Grab one more hot memory to sustain her through the difficult truth she would have to face when she got home?

This was her holiday of a lifetime, after all, and Cooper Delaney—toy boy extraordinaire—her passport to no-holds-barred pleasure.

She relaxed, warmed by the comfort of his embrace. 'All right, but I'll go soon.'

Her lips tilted into a smile as he grunted. 'Shut up and go to sleep.' His forearm tightened under her breasts. 'You're going to need to get your strength up, my little cougar. This toy boy isn't finished with you yet.'

She choked out a laugh—that became a wistful hum as his arm became slack and her own body drifted towards sleep.

Colourful images collected behind her eyes—the glitter of pink sand beaches, the darting sparkle of blue-finned fish, the tangerine glow of fruit juice and rum, and the piercing jade of Cooper Delaney's eyes.

She swallowed to relieve the clutching sensation in her chest, and tumbled headlong into the rainbow dream.

CHAPTER FIVE

'HEY, COOP, GET your butt out of bed, it's past eleven. And I've got exciting news.'

The muffled musical voice intruded on Ella's dream. She squeezed open an eyelid, grateful when the brittle sunlight hitting her retinas didn't appear to be accompanied by any pain, despite the definite thumping in her head.

Flopping over onto her back, she squinted at the empty bed beside her, the rumpled sheets striped by the sunlight slanting through the shutters. And heard the thumping again. This time, though, it was definitely not in her head, but coming from the hut's door, which shook on its hinges as the same musical voice from her dream, lilting with the lazy rhythms of a Bermuda native, shouted: 'No use hiding, man. Henry told me you'd be here.'

Ella shot upright, clasping the bed's thin sheet to her naked breasts, and swayed as several questions bombarded her at once.

How long had she been asleep? Where were her clothes? Where was Coop? And who the heck was that woman banging on the door?

The answer to number one was hours, if the brightness of the sunlight was anything to go by. Scrambling out of bed as furtively as possible, she located her clothes in a neatly stacked pile on the arm of the sagging sofa, answering question number two. Questions three and four remained a mystery though, as she dressed as soundlessly as she could manage while continuing to scan the hut for any sign of her host.

She jumped as the banging began again.

'Hey, I can hear you in there. Avoidance won't do you a damn bit of good.'

Rats, do you have bionic hearing?

She waited a few more strained seconds, while debating opening the shutters and escaping onto the deck, but eventually discarded the idea—given the girl's hearing capabilities.

The banging continued, and her not entirely settled stomach churned. What if this girl were Cooper's girlfriend? Or his wife? Was that why he'd disappeared? Because what did she really know about Captain Studly, except that he was gorgeous, knew how to dance the soca and had magic fingers, a very inventive tongue, and a huge and permanently stiff...

Don't go there.

Squaring her shoulders, she swung the door open ready to face the consequences, to be greeted by a stunningly beautiful barefoot young woman of about twenty, wearing a pair of Daisy Dukes, a T-shirt with the message 'Don't Mess with a Libran', tightly braided hair decorated with multicoloured beads, and a stunned expression.

'Hi.' She craned her neck to search the hut's interior, having gained her composure a lot faster than Ella. 'Is Coop around?'

'Um, no, apparently not,' Ella replied, opting for the only answer she could give with any confidence.

'Uh-huh?' The girl gave her a thorough once-over that had the heat steaming into Ella's cheeks. 'I guess he's up at the big house.'

The big house? What big house?

'Sorry to wake you,' the girl said. 'Henry didn't tell me

Coop left the Runner with company last night. Just that he headed for his beach hut. Suppose Henry was messing with me. And Coop.'

And me, thought Ella, annoyed by Henry the barman's joke, and acutely embarrassed that this girl now knew she was the sort of woman who got picked up in bars.

What had seemed wildly romantic last night, now felt pretty tacky.

Ruby had encouraged her to let her inner flirt loose, but there had definitely been no mention of getting tipsy on rum cocktails, then getting nekkid with Captain Studly and jumping him four...no, five...oh, heck, make that at least a half-dozen times during the night.

'You Coop's new lady?' The girl interrupted Ella's panicked reappraisal of her behaviour.

'Um, no, we're just...' *What? Snorkel mates? Dance partners? Bonk buddies?*

The burning in her cheeks promptly hit maximum voltage as she searched for the appropriate term while recalling in X-rated detail exactly how intimately she and the invisible Coop had got acquainted last night, after very little provocation. 'Friends,' she finished lamely.

With benefits. Gold-standard benefits.

The phrase hung in the brisk morning air unspoken, but not unfigured out if the girl's frank appraisal was anything to go by. 'Do you know when he's going to be back?'

Hardly, seeing as I have no clue where he is.

'I'm afraid not.'

'Could you tell him I stopped by? I'm Sonny's daughter, Josie, and I—'

'Why don't you come in and wait for him?' Ella shoved the door wide, determined to make a fast getaway, before this situation got any more awkward. 'I was just leaving.'

Josie sent her a doubtful look as she stepped into the room. 'You sure, I—'

'Absolutely positive,' Ella replied, grabbing her bag from the hook by the door and slipping past the girl, before she could ask any more unanswerable questions.

'You want me to give Coop a message?'

Ella paused on the porch, the clutching sensation she'd had as she fell asleep the night before returning. 'Would you tell him thanks?' She cleared her throat, the stupid clutching sensation starting to squeeze her ribcage.

For being a friend when I needed one, she added silently as she jumped off the hut's porch and her feet sank into the wet sand.

Josie called out a goodbye and she waved back as she set off down the beach. But she didn't glance back again. Knowing it would only tighten the band squeezing her chest.

She'd had an amazing night. Maybe she'd gone a little off piste from Ruby's plan—and discovered the liberating powers of flirtation, soca dancing, Rum Swizzles and sweaty, no-strings sex in the process. Okay, make that a lot off piste.

But it was all good.

Give or take the odd heart murmur.

'Up you get, Sleeping Beauty, breakfast is served.' Coop bumped the hut's door open with his butt, keeping a firm hold on the tray his housekeeper had piled high with freshly sliced fruit, French toast, syrup and coffee. It had taken Inez a good half hour to assemble everything to her exacting standards—and quiz him mercilessly about his 'overnight guest'—during which time he'd got stupidly eager to see Ella again. Enough to question why he hadn't just woken her up and invited her to his place for breakfast.

The fifteen-acre estate that overlooked the cove, and the two-storey colonial he'd built on the bluff, were a symbol of who he was now. And he was super proud of it—and all he'd achieved, after ten long, back-breaking years of dawn wake-up calls refurbing second-hand equipment, long days spent out on the ocean running back-to-back dives, late nights getting his brain in a knot at the local community college studying for his MBA, all while keeping a ready smile on his face to schmooze a succession of tourists and corporate clients and bank managers and investors.

His business—Dive Guys—had made its first million-dollar turnover five years ago, and he'd celebrated by buying himself a brand-new motor launch, and the beach hut he'd been renting since his early days with Sonny. Three years later, he'd expanded the franchise across the Caribbean and had finally had enough to invest in the construction of his dream home on the land he'd bought behind the hut. He'd moved into Half-Moon House two years ago— but still couldn't quite believe that all those years of work had paid off in a wraparound deck that looked out over the ocean, five luxury en-suite bedrooms, a forty-foot infinity pool, a mile of private beach and an extremely nosey housekeeper.

Normally, he loved showing the place off to women he dated.

But when he'd woken up with Ella cuddled in his arms, he'd decided to keep the place a secret until after he'd finessed Inez into cooking a lavish breakfast for his overnight guest.

There had been something so cute and refreshing about Ella's breathless enthusiasm when she'd got a load of his first place the night before. She wasn't the only woman he'd brought to the hut, but she was the only one who had appreciated its charm and overlooked the used furniture and lack of amenities.

For some weird reason it had felt good to know all she'd seen was him—not Dive Guys, or the things it had afforded him.

'That looks real tasty, Coop. You shouldn't have bothered, though—I already grabbed a crab patty up at the
Runner.'

Coop swung round, nearly dropping the tray, to find
Sonny's daughter, Josie, perched on one of his bar stools.
With her long legs crossed at the knee and a mocking
smile on her lips, she should have looked all grown up,
but somehow all he ever saw was the fresh kid he'd met a
decade ago and who had made it her mission in life to be
a thorn in his side ever since.

'Josie, what are you doing here?' He dumped the tray on
the counter, sloshing the coffee all over the French toast, as
he took in the empty bed in the far corner, and the empty
couch where he'd folded Ella's clothes into a pile not more
than thirty minutes ago. 'And where the hell is Ella?'

Josie's grin became smug as she snagged a chunk of
fresh pineapple off the breakfast tray. 'So that's Sleeping
Beauty's name. I always wondered if she had one.'

'Ha, ha,' he said without heat, used to Josie's teasing.

'She's very pretty. But kind of shy. Not your usual type.'

'Where is she?' he asked again, not happy at the news
that Josie had met her. Somehow he didn't think someone
with Ella's insta-blush tendencies would appreciate being
caught in his bed by a smartass like Josie. 'Please tell me
you didn't say anything to make her bolt.'

Josie sucked on the pineapple, shaking her head. 'Uh-
uh. She bolted all on her own. Seemed kind of spooked
that you'd disappeared.'

He ran his fingers through his hair. Damn it, he'd only
been gone a half-hour and Ella had looked totally done
in. After the workout they'd both had last night he would
have bet she'd be comatose for hours yet. The thought had
him eyeing his uninvited guest. 'You woke her up, didn't
you, you little…?'

He made a swipe for Josie, but she leapt off the stool

and danced out of his reach, laughing. 'What's the big deal? You don't date the tourists, remember? In case they get ideas.'

Not Ella.

The thought popped into his head, and had him stopping dead in front of Josie—the quest for retribution dying a quick death.

What was with that? Sure Ella had been sweet, and eager and inventive in bed, but how had she got under his guard so easily? Knowing what he did about tourists who liked to slum it in neighbourhood bars, how come he had never thought of Ella as one of them? And why had he crept out of bed and harassed Inez into making her breakfast? He didn't have a romantic bone in his body. Not since...

He stared at the ruined toast, the creeping sense of humiliation coming back in an unpleasant rush of memory.

Not since the evening of the junior prom in Garysville, Indiana, when he'd stood like a dummy on Amy Metcalfe's porch, his neck burning under the collar of the borrowed suit, and a corsage clutched in his sweating palm that had cost him ten of his hard-earned dollars, while Amy's old man yelled at him to get lost, and his prom date sent him a pitying smile from the passenger seat of his half-brother Jack Jnr's Beemer convertible.

'Don't you want to know why I'm here?' Josie stared at him, her usual mischief replaced with excitement. 'I've got news.'

Shaking off the unpleasant memory, he clamped down hard on the dumb urge to head out after Ella. 'Sure? What news?' He tossed a piece of papaya into his mouth, impressed with his own nonchalance.

The smile on Josie's face reached ear-to-ear proportions. 'Taylor popped the question last night and I said yes.'

'What question?' he said, trying to process the information while his mind was still snagged on Ella and why the hell she'd run out on him. Wasn't Taylor that pimply kid Josie'd been dating for a while?

Josie's eyes rounded. 'Damn, Coop, even you can't be that dumb. The "Will you marry me?" question. Duh.'

Coop choked on the mango chunk he'd just slung in his mouth. 'You've got to be kidding me?' His eyes watered as his aggravation over Ella's sudden departure was surpassed by horror. 'You're way too young to be getting married.' Plus marriage was for chumps—and Josie was a smart kid—what was she thinking?

Josie whacked him hard on the back, dislodging the chunk and nearly dislocating his shoulder. 'I'm twenty,' she said, indignantly. 'Taylor and I have been dating for four years.' She propped her hands on her hips, striking the Wonder Woman pose he knew meant she was about to start lecturing him. 'And we love each other. Marriage is the obvious next step. So we can think about babies.'

'Babies!' he yelped, as a blood vessel popped out on his forehead and began to throb. 'You cannot be serious?'

'Just because you're dead set on being the Oldest Player in Town,' she countered, 'doesn't mean everyone's that cynical and immature.'

'I'm immature?' he snapped. Seeing her flinch, he struggled to lower his voice, and regain some of his usual cool.

But damn it, first Ella's disappearing act, and now this? Had all the females in Bermuda been hitting the crazy sauce while he slept?

'Honey, I'm not the one planning to get hitched when I'm still in college.' Not to mention have a parcel of rugrats. Was she nuts?

The look she sent him went from pissed to pitying. 'Why does the thought of that terrify you so much, Coop? Maybe you should try it some time yourself?'

'What? Marriage? And kids?' he scoffed, barely suppressing the shudder. 'No way.'

'Not that, not yet, but…' Josie searched his face, the pitying look starting to annoy him now. 'Couldn't you at least try dating the same woman for longer than a week?' Her eyes shadowed with concern. 'Haven't you ever thought there might be more to women than just hot and sweaty sex?'

'Damn it, give me a break.' He slapped his hands over his ears. 'Don't talk to me about that stuff—my ears are bleeding.' He'd never kept his dating habits a secret, but Josie butting into his sex life was just wrong. On so many levels.

She glared at him. 'So who's being immature now?'

He dropped his hands, having to concede that point. 'Fine, you win that one, but conversations about sex are off limits, okay?' The last thing he needed was some snot-nosed kid giving him dating advice.

'Okay, truce.' She surprised him by backing down. 'I'll butt out of your business. You're a hopeless cause anyway.' She sighed, to emphasise the point. 'I didn't come here to argue with you, I came to tell you Taylor and I want to set the date for August tenth. If you're good with us using your land to do the ceremony on the cove near the Runner?'

'Sure, of course, no problem,' he said, feeling about two feet tall all of a sudden. He hadn't meant to piss on her parade; the wedding announcement had just come as a shock, that was all. How the heck had Josie grown up without him noticing?

'I also wanted to ask you to be my witness,' she added. 'If you think you can contain your horror long enough to sign the book?' The shadow of uncertainty in her gaze shaved another foot off his stature. Hell, he hadn't meant to be that much of a grouch.

'You sure you want the Oldest Player in Town there?' he murmured, relieved when she sent him a cheeky grin.

'Only if he promises not to hit on the bridesmaids.'

The thought of hitting on anyone brought back thoughts of Ella. And the pang of regret sliced under his ribs. She had to be long gone by now.

He raised his hand as if taking a mock oath. 'I do solemnly swear not to hit on the bridesmaids.'

'Cool, we're all set, then.' Josie grinned, then planted a kiss on the tip of his nose. 'I'll keep you posted on the wedding plans. I better hit the road, though.' She rolled her eyes. 'You have no idea how much work goes into organising a wedding in under four months.'

And he didn't want to know, he thought silently, but decided to keep that information to himself.

'Oh, by the way,' she said as she reached the door. 'Sleeping Beauty left you a message before she ran off.'

'Yeah?' The bubble of hope expanded under his breastbone. 'What message? Did she tell you where she's staying?' Maybe if she had, he could give her a call? Get Inez to make a fresh batch of French toast, or better yet some lunch?

Josie shook her head. 'She just said to tell you thanks.'

'That's it?' The bubble of hope deflated, making his voice sound flat and dull.

Josie nodded, her expression thoughtful as she studied him. 'If you wanted to contact her, Henry might know where she's staying if she was at the Runner last night. You know how talkative he is.'

'No, that's okay, it's no big deal,' he replied, and willed himself to believe it.

'Are you sure?'

He forced out a laugh. 'Sure, I'm sure. Not my style.' He didn't get hung up on women, even ones as cute and sexy as Ella. 'Oldest Player in Town, remember?'

Josie rolled her eyes again. 'Oh, yeah. How could I forget?'

But after Josie had left, and he had dumped the ruined breakfast spread in the trash and collapsed onto the bed, the joke nickname didn't seem all that funny any more. Especially when he got a lungful of the light, refreshing, lemony scent and the earthy smell of sex that still lingered on the sheets.

CHAPTER SIX

ELLA PLUCKED THE TRAY of Triple Indulgence Brownies out of the industrial oven and dropped it gingerly on the counter—her tummy hitching up towards her throat as the aroma of melting chocolate surrounded her. The rich decadent scent tasted like charcoal on her tongue. Clasping her hand over her mouth, she sliced the brownies into twelve chunks, perched the tray on the window sill to cool, and rushed into the café, her stomach wobbling alarmingly.

Taking deep, measured breaths, she berated herself and her stupid nervous tummy as she stacked the batch of mini-chocolate tarts she'd made earlier—which thankfully didn't smell too strongly. Ruby would be here any minute and the last thing she needed was more searching looks and probing questions from her business partner—because she'd barfed all over the shop again.

She'd been tense and out of sorts for weeks. Ever since she'd got back from Bermuda and got the diagnosis she'd been dreading from her doctor, Myra Patel. That she was no longer ovulating at regular intervals—which explained the now five months without a period—because the onset of premature menopause was now a reality.

But she thought she'd come to terms with it. Or at least found a strategy to deal with her loss. Even though her biological clock was now ticking at triple time—and Myra had told her that her chances of conceiving naturally were probably remote, and getting remoter by the second—she had referred her to a specialist. Plus she and Ruby had discussed the feasibility of other options, when and if she found a life partner.

The good news was, after her wild night with Coop, there was every reason to be a lot more cheerful about her prospects when it came to relationships. Or at least sexual relationships.

Coop.

Her stomach clutched and released, the queasiness returning.

Maybe it was about time she admitted that her fertility problems weren't the only thing that had had her down in the dumps? That her nervous stomach wasn't just a symptom of her stress over the test results she'd got from Myra two months ago, but also her ridiculous overreaction to her one night with Cooper Delaney.

Somehow, she'd got fixated on him, picking over every minute detail of their day and night together—instead of assigning the experience to its rightful place in her past, and moving on with her real life.

So what if he'd disappeared the following morning, without leaving a note to say where he'd gone? They'd had a one-night fling. He'd owed her nothing. They lived thousands of miles apart, and he was only twenty-eight, for goodness' sake. Not that their age difference had bothered him... Then again, maybe it had, more than he'd let on. Could that be why he'd disappeared so abruptly? Before she'd even woken up? Without bothering to say goodbye?

She folded the oven mitt she'd used into the drawer and slammed it shut.

Stop right there, you're doing it again.

The hollow feeling of inadequacy opened up in her stomach, and the weary ache in her chest pinched her heart.

Maybe if she had left him a note...

She sighed and glanced up to see Ruby and Cal standing together on the pavement outside the shop—bidding
each other goodbye as they did every morning before Cal
headed for the tube station and his work as a top defence
barrister in the City. The hollow weight became a gaping
hole as she watched them.

Ruby threw her head back and laughed at something
her husband had said. Callum said something else, that
seemed to make her laugh more, but then he gripped the
lapels of her coat and jerked her up onto her tiptoes, before
silencing the laughter with a hungry kiss.

Ella felt the nasty dart of envy as Ruby's arms wrapped
around Cal's neck to pull him closer. The kiss heated to
scorching, Cal's hands finding Ruby's bottom beneath
the hem of her coat. Anyone passing by would have mistaken them for newlyweds, instead of a couple who had
recently celebrated their seventh wedding anniversary and
had three very energetic children ranging in age from two
to six.

Ella dropped her chin, and concentrated on rearrang-
ing the cookies on the display, feeling like a Peeping Tom
as the nausea pitched and rolled in her belly. The door-
bell tinkled, then the creak of the café door opened and
slammed shut followed by the click of Ruby's stilettos on
the tiled floor.

'Sorry I'm late. I'll close up today to make up for it.'
Ruby's voice sounded upbeat and pleasantly mellow, as it
often did first thing in the morning. Ella frowned, dust-
ing icing sugar over the tarts. Hard to remember now that
her business partner had once been the biggest grump on
the planet until she'd downed at least two cups of coffee
in the morning, but that was before her fender bender with
Callum Westmore nearly eight years ago.

'That man sweet-talked me back into bed,' Ruby added
with a huff. 'After Helga picked up the kids.'

'Poor you,' Ella muttered under her breath, then bit her lip to contain the sour note of sarcasm, and the bile rising up her throat.

What was the matter with her? She'd always been so happy for Ruby and Cal. It wasn't as if their path to true love had exactly been smooth. And as for Max and Ally and Art, Ruby and Cal's three irrepressible children, she adored them. And adored having a special place in their lives as their favourite 'auntie'. That relationship would only become more treasured if the possibility of a childless future became a reality.

'Ella, is everything okay?'

She put down the icing sugar to find Ruby watching her. Far too closely. Oh, no. Had she just heard that cutting remark? How was she supposed to explain it? 'Yes, of course...'

'Are you sure? You're a rather strange colour.'

'Really, I'm perfectly—' The gag reflex struck without warning, punching Ella's larynx and slamming her stomach into her throat. She slapped her hand over her mouth, and raced around the counter and into the restroom—getting there just in time to lose in the toilet the tea and dry toast she'd managed to force down that morning for breakfast.

'Okay, deep breaths.' Ruby rubbed Ella's spine as the nausea retreated. The cool cloth felt glorious on the back of her neck as she dragged in several deep breaths.

'How's your stomach? All finished puking?'

'Yes, I think so.' Ella pressed her hand to her belly to double-check. But her stomach seemed to have settled after the retching, the strong scent of the disinfectant in the toilet nowhere near as abrasive as the brownie scent had been earlier.

Ruby flushed the toilet and anchored her arm around Ella's waist. 'Good, then let's get you more comfortable.'

By the time they'd both settled in the two armchairs at the back of the café, Ruby's careful scrutiny had Ella's cheeks burning.

'Any idea what caused it?' Ruby asked.

Ella took a moment to examine the hands she had clasped in her lap.

'From that delightful shade of rosé on your cheeks I'm guessing you do know.' Ruby's hand covered hers and squeezed. 'But you don't want to say.'

'It's silly.' Ella shrugged, forced to face her friend. 'I'm totally overreacting to a stupid holiday fling—which didn't mean anything.'

'Of course it meant something. You wouldn't have slept with him if it didn't. You're not the casual-sex type.'

Ella breathed a heavy sigh. 'Kind of annoying that I didn't figure that out before I decided to jump into bed with him for a night of casual sex, isn't it?' The clutching sensation in her chest was back with a vengeance. 'I miss him. I wish I'd hung around to tell him goodbye properly. Got closure. Then maybe I could stop giving myself an ulcer thinking about him constantly.'

Ruby nodded, her expression far too intuitive. 'All excellent points. But can I suggest another possible explanation for the puking?'

Ella frowned. Why was Ruby looking at her like that? As if she was struggling to suppress a smile. 'There is no other—'

'Because you're no more the highly strung, give-yourself-an-ulcer type than you are the casual-sex type.'

'Your point?' Ella replied a little sharply.

'Look, you've been stressing about your holiday fling for weeks, I know that. But isn't it at all possible—given the extremely hot description you gave me of your bedroom aerobics with Captain Studly—that what we just witnessed might be something more substantial than a nervous tummy?'

'Such as?'

'Morning sickness.'

Ella stiffened. 'You know that's not possible.'

'According to Dr Patel it isn't impossible.'

Ella's frown became a scowl. 'It's only a very slight possibility. And we used condoms the whole time.'

'As did Cal and I before we got pregnant with Arturo,' Ruby shot straight back.

'It's not the same thing.' The sour note was back. 'You don't have any fertility issues.'

'I still think you should do a pregnancy test, just to be sure.'

Ella straightened in the chair. 'I am sure.' Sure what the result would be. And even surer that bringing back memories of another pregnancy test that she'd taken with Ruby years before would only make her current misery seem even more insurmountable.

'Well, I'm not.'

Ella threw up her hands. 'Yes, well, I don't have a pregnancy test and I don't have time to go and get one because we open in half an hour.' Maybe if Ruby wouldn't listen to her, at least she'd listen to reason.

'That's okay, because I do.' Reaching into her handbag, Ruby produced a blue and white chemist bag from which she pulled out a telltale pink box.

'Where did you get that?' Ella stared, her hurt and astonishment turning to dismay.

'Ella, you've been sick three times this week now.' Grabbing Ella's hand, Ruby slapped the box into her palm.

Ella wanted to refuse, but as she stared at the box she felt her will power crumbling in the face of Ruby's determination.

'Just go pee on the stick.' Ruby closed Ella's fingers around the box. 'Don't overthink this. Whatever the result is, we'll handle it. But denial is not the answer. I'll wait here.'

Ella stood up, her stomach folding in on itself, as the last of her will power ebbed away on a wave of exhaustion. 'Okay, fine, but you may be waiting a long time.' She frowned at her best friend. 'I am so not in the mood to pee on demand right now.'

It took fifteen torturous minutes before she could get out of the toilet.

'I left it on the vanity in there.' She washed her hands in the shop's sink and dosed them with anti-bacterial gel. 'Don't forget to dispose of it before we open,' she added, brushing the stupid sting of tears off her cheek.

'Ella, don't cry. You need to know for sure.'

She didn't dignify that with an answer, but simply set about filling the icing bag with cream-cheese frosting. She needed to be ready for the nine a.m. rush when they opened in fifteen minutes. She so did not have time for this rubbish.

She was still busy adding cream-cheese frosting in decorative swirls to the carrot cake when Ruby dashed back into the café a few minutes later. 'I think you better look at this.'

'Don't bring it in here,' she said crossly. 'It's covered in pee.'

'I know that,' Ruby replied. 'But it's not just any pee, it's pregnant-lady pee.'

'What?' Frosting squirted across the counter as her fingers fisted on the bag involuntarily. And her heart jumped into her mouth.

'You heard me.' Ruby held the pee stick in front of Ella's face like a talisman. 'See that strong blue line? That means

Ella's going to be a mummy in exactly seven months' time. You're going to be ringing in the new year with your very own bundle of fun.'

She couldn't focus, thanks to the sheen of shocked tears misting her vision. 'But that's not possible,' she murmured, her voice hoarse.

Ruby laughed. 'Um, well, clearly it is. Pregnancy tests don't lie.'

Ella's unfocused gaze raised to Ruby's smiling face. 'I should take another one. It might be wrong.'

'Take as many as you like, but there's no such thing as a false positive with these things. I took six tests with Art. And they all came out exactly the same. Assuming it was definitely you who peed on that stick, it's definitely you who's pregnant.'

Ella collapsed into the chair beside the cash register. Her knees trembling now almost as violently as her hands— which clutched the bag of frosting in a death grip as it dripped onto the floor.

'I'm going to have a baby.' The words sounded fragile and far away, as if they had been said by someone else, as if they could be extinguished if she said them too loudly.

Ruby stroked her back as she crouched beside her and wrapped her hand round Ella's wrist. 'Yes, you are.'

The tears welled and flowed, her whole body shaking now, at the memory of a similar test so long ago. The joy then had felt scary, terrifying, but so small and sweet. This time it didn't feel small, it felt huge, like a living, breathing thing that couldn't be contained within her skin, but so much more scary and terrifying too.

Dumping the pregnancy test in the bin, Ruby washed and dried her hands, then tugged a couple of wet wipes from the dispenser on the counter. 'I take it those are happy tears?' Ruby took the icing bag out of Ella's numb fingers and began cleaning the mess of cream-cheese frosting with the wipes.

Ella nodded, the lump in her throat too solid and overwhelming to talk around.

'Am I allowed to say I told you so, then?'

Ella's eyes focused at last, and she swept her arms round her friend's shoulders and clung on tight, too overwhelmed to care about the smug smile on Ruby's face.

'I don't deserve this chance.' She sobbed as Ruby hugged her.

Ruby moved back, and held her arms. 'Don't say that.' She gave her a slight shake. 'What you did then, you did for the right reasons.'

Ella folded her arms over her stomach, as if to protect the precious life within and stop the guilt from consuming the joy. 'I'm not so sure about that.'

Ruby tugged a tissue out of her pocket, to dab at Ella's eyes. 'You were eighteen years old Ella, you had your whole life ahead of you, and it was a mistake. You made the only choice you could in the circumstances.' She placed the damp tissue in the palm of Ella's hand, rolled her fist over it, and held on. 'Don't you think it's about time to forgive yourself?'

She would never be able to forgive herself, not completely, but that didn't mean she couldn't protect this child with every fibre of her being. This time she wouldn't mess it up. 'I want to.'

Ruby's lips quirked. 'Okay, next question. Because I'm going to assume the "Do you want to have this baby?" question is a no-brainer.'

Ella bobbed her head as the small smile spread. 'Yes, it is.'

'Brilliant. So next question, how do we contact Captain Studly? Do you have like a card for his tour company or something?'

'What? No.' The joy cracked, like the crumbling top of a newly baked muffin, exposing the soft centre beneath. 'We can't tell him. He doesn't need to know.'

'Calm down.' Ruby gripped her fingers tight. 'There's no need to panic. You don't have to do anything yet.'

The memory of his voice, smooth, seductive, husky, and so sexy asking, 'Are you on the pill?' seemed to float in the air around the café, mocking her.

What happened if she told him and he reacted the same way Randall had? He was still in his twenties; he lived in a beach hut; he picked up women in bars. He was exciting, reckless, charming, sexier than any one she'd ever met, and probably the least likely guy on the planet to welcome news like this.

'And he's not necessarily going to freak out the way Randall did,' Ruby said, doing her mind-reading thing.

Oh, yes, he will.

'I don't want to risk it.' She tugged her hands out of Ruby's. 'Why do I have to tell him?'

'Because it's his baby, and he has a right to know,' Ruby said, in that patient I-know-what's-best voice that she'd acquired ever since having kids. Ella had always thought it was so sweet. Now she was finding it more than a little patronising.

'But suppose he'd rather not know?'

'How can you possibly know that?' Ruby replied.

She opened her mouth to tell Ruby how he'd asked her if she was on the pill and how the correct answer had somehow got lost in the heat of the moment. But then shut it again. She didn't want Ruby to think she'd deliberately tricked him, because she hadn't. But even thinking about that conversation now made her feel as if she had, which would only tarnish the perfection of this moment.

'He lives in Bermuda. I don't need his support.' Especially as he didn't have any money. 'I'm more than solvent on my own and—'

'That's not the point. He's the baby's father. By not telling him you're not giving him the choice, or the baby the choice to know him when it gets older. Think of how much it screwed up Nick when he found out our dad wasn't his biological father,' she said, reminding Ella of her brother Nick, who had run away from home in his teens when he'd discovered the truth about his parentage and had only recently come back into Ruby's life.

'It's not the same thing at all,' Ella protested. It wasn't as if she planned never to tell her child who its father was; she just didn't see why she had to tell the father right this second.

'I know it's not, but what I'm trying to say is you can't keep those kinds of secrets. It's not fair on either one of them.'

Ella wanted to say life wasn't fair. But the truth was she'd never believed that. Life could be fair, if you made the effort to make it so.

She wanted to deny he had any right to know. This was her child. Her responsibility. And she didn't want to consider his rights, his reaction. But even as the panic sat under her breastbone, ready to leap up her throat and cut off her air supply, she pictured Coop's face, the genuine smile, those emerald eyes twinkling with humour, and knew that not telling him would be taking the coward's way out.

While she never would have planned to have a child alone, that was what she'd be doing—because fate had handed her this incredible gift. And while it was very likely that Coop wouldn't want to know about this baby, she had to at least give him the option of saying no. Because she had to give her child the chance to know its father. However slim that chance might be.

Ruby patted her hand. 'How about we leave this discussion for another day? You really don't have to do this yet.'

A loud tapping had them both turning to see the whole of the Hampstead Heath Mother and Baby Stroller Work-Out Class crowded around the door, looking sweaty and dishevelled and in desperate need of light refreshments.

Jumping up, Ella headed round the counter, to flip the sign on the door to open and welcome them in. As they smiled and wheeled their babies proudly into the café, chatting about the Hitler who ran the class, Ella smiled back, amazed to realise the lethagy that had dragged her down for days had vanished.

'Wait, Ella, are you sure you don't want to go home and rest? I can handle the Yummies,' Ruby offered as she joined her behind the counter.

Ella grinned back at her, the ball of panic lifting too.

She had time to think about how to tell Cooper; how to break the news to him without making him feel responsible. And really, while the thought of what she had to tell him wasn't easy, the fact that she had a reason to speak to him again felt surprisingly good. 'No need. I feel great.'

Ruby laughed back, her own face beaming with pleasure. 'Just wait till tomorrow morning when you're crouched over the toilet bowl again. Actually, we better get some buckets for the duration.'

Ella spent the morning chatting to the mums, serving tea and freshly baked cakes and cookies, whipping up a succession of speciality coffees, while she admired their children, and struggled to contain the silly grin at how totally amazing her life suddenly was.

She'd speak to Cooper soon. Ruby was right: it would be wrong not to. But it had been an accident. And really, she didn't need to think about all the particulars just yet. Right now, all she really had to do was bask in the miracle occurring inside her. And focus on making sure she gave her baby the best possible chance to thrive. And if that meant eventually finding the courage to tell its father about their happy accident, she'd do it, somehow.

CHAPTER SEVEN

'Ouch. Damn it!' Coop yanked his hand out of the casing, and threw the wrench down on the deck. Blood seeped from the shallow gash at the base of his thumb, through the thick black smear of engine grease. He sucked on it, getting a mouthful of grit to go with the metallic taste of his own blood.

'What's all the cussing for?' Sonny's head peered out from the captain's cabin.

'That damn propeller just took a chunk out of my hand,' he snarled. 'Cussing's required.' He boosted himself onto the deck. Tying the rag he'd been using to clean off the drive shaft around the injury, he sent his friend an angry glare. 'That lug nut won't budge—probably because it's been rusted on for thirty years.' With his hand now pounding in unison with his head, after one too many drinks last night at The Rum Runner, he was not in the mood to be dicking around with Sonny's ancient outboard motor.

Sonny tilted his head to one side, sending him a calm, searching look. 'Someone sure got out of bed the wrong way again this morning.'

Coop ignored the jibe. So what if he hadn't been on top form lately? Ever since a certain English girl had left him high and dry, her lush body and eager smile had got lodged in his frontal lobe and it had been interfering with his sleep patterns.

Going back to The Rum Runner last night for the first time since Ella had run out on him had been a mistake. Henry had started jerking his chain about 'his pretty lady', and he'd somehow ended up challenging the guy to a drinking contest. Staggering home at three a.m., and being violently ill in his bathroom had only added injury to the insult of too many tequila slammers and too many nights without enough sleep.

No wonder he wasn't at his sunniest.

'Isn't it about time you got rid of this bucket?' he said, letting out a little of his frustration on Sonny's boat.

Sonny stroked the console with the affection most men reserved for a lover. 'My *Jezebel*'s got plenty good years in her yet. And with Josie's wedding to pay for, she's going to have to make them count.'

Coop knotted the rag with his teeth, his temper kicking in. They both knew *The Jezebel* hadn't seen a good year since Bill Clinton had been in the White House. And that he'd offered to bankroll Josie's wedding a million times and Sonny had stubbornly refused to accept the money. But after a morning spent with a raging hangover trying to fix the unfixable when he should have been going over his business manager's projections for the new franchise in Acapulco, he wasn't in the mood to keep his reservations about Josie's nuptials to himself any longer either.

'What is Josie getting hitched for anyway? She's only twenty and they're both still in college. What are they going to live on?'

'Love will find a way,' Sonny replied with that proud paternal grin that had been rubbing Coop the wrong way for weeks. Hadn't the old guy figured out yet he was shelling out a king's ransom to kick-start a marriage that probably wouldn't last out the year?

'Will it?' he asked, the edge in his voice going razor sharp.

Sonny nodded, the probing look sending prickles of unease up Coop's spine and making his thumb throb. 'You know, you've been mighty bitchy for months now. Wanna tell me what's going on?'

Months? No way had it been months since his night with Ella. Had it? 'This isn't about me, Sonny,' he said, struggling to deflect the conversation back where it needed to be. 'This is about Josie doing something dumb and you not lifting a finger to stop her.'

'Josie's known her own mind since she was three years old,' Sonny said without any heat. 'Nothing I could say would stop her even if I wanted to.'

Coop opened his mouth to protest, but Sonny simply lifted up a silencing finger.

'But I don't want to stop them. Taylor's a good kid and she loves him. And it's not them I'm worried about.' Sonny rested his heavy frame on the bench next to Coop, his steady gaze making the prickles on Coop's spine feel as if he'd been rolling in poison ivy. 'You're the one hasn't been right ever since the night you picked up that tourist girl in the Runner.'

'What the...?' Coop's jaw went slack. How did Sonny know about Ella? The old guy was always butting into his personal life, because he was a romantic and he thought he had a right to. But he'd never spoken about Ella to anyone. Did Sonny have X-ray vision or something?

'Josie says you seemed real taken with her the next morning. But she'd run off? Is that the thing? You miss her?'

Damn Josie—so she was his source.

'It's not what you think.' Coop scowled, trying to cut the old guy off at the pass before this conversation got totally out of hand.

He didn't miss Ella, and he wasn't 'taken with her'. Whatever the heck that meant. It was nothing like that.

She'd just got under his skin, somehow. Like an itch he couldn't scratch. He could wait it out. Give it a couple more weeks and surely the almost nightly dreams he had, about those bright blue eyes wide with enthusiasm, that sunny smile, that lush butt in the itsy-bitsy purple bikini...

He thrust his fingers through his hair, annoyed by the low-level heat humming in his crotch as the erotic memories spun gleefully back—and the weird knot under his breastbone twisted.

'It was a one-night hook-up,' he continued, trying to convince himself now as much as Sonny. 'We hit it off. But only...you know.'

Just shoot me now.

He shrugged. He wasn't about to get into a discussion about his sex life with Sonny. The old guy had given him chapter and verse as a teenager about respecting women, and he didn't need that lecture again. One thing was certain, though: Josie was dead meat next time he saw her for putting him in this position. Whether she had a ten-grand wedding to attend in five weeks or not.

'I don't think Ella and I are going to be declaring any vows,' he said, going on the defensive when Sonny gave him that look that always made him feel as if he had a case to answer.

He did respect women. He respected them a lot. Sonny just had a quaint, old-fashioned idea that sex always had to mean something. When sometimes all it meant was you needed to get laid.

'She lives thousands of miles away, we only spent one night together and she wasn't looking for anything more than I was. Plus she was the one who ran out on me.'

Sonny's eyebrow winged up, and Coop knew he'd said too much.

'I see. So you're the boy that can have any woman he

wants. And she's the girl that didn't want you? Is that what's got you so upset?'

'I'm not upset.' Coop flexed his fist, his hand hurting like a son of a bitch. 'And thanks a bunch for making me sound like an arrogant jackass.'

Sonny smiled, but didn't deny it, and Coop felt the flicker of hurt. 'You're a good-looking boy with more money than you need and a charming way about you that draws women like bees to a honeypot. You've got a right to be arrogant, I guess.'

'Thanks,' Coop said wryly. He didn't kid himself, Sonny hadn't meant it as a compliment.

Money wasn't something that floated Sonny's boat; it was the one thing they still argued about. Because as far as Coop was concerned, money mattered, more than pretty much everything else. It made everything easier, oiled every cog, gave you options, and that all-important safety net that he'd lacked as a kid. He'd craved it for the first twenty years of his life. But now he had it, it meant more to him than just the luxuries, or the good times he could buy with it. It meant respect. Status. It showed people that he wasn't the worthless little trailer-trash nobody he'd once been. But best of all it meant he didn't have to rely on anyone but himself.

He liked Sonny, respected the guy more than any other guy he had ever known, but, the way he saw it, Sonny had way too many responsibilities in his life—to his five kids, his three grandkids, all his friends and acquaintances, not to mention Rhona, the wife he'd had by his side for over thirty years. Maybe that worked for Sonny, he certainly didn't seem to mind it, but, as far as Coop was concerned, that wasn't something he was looking for. A man could be an island—if he worked hard enough and had enough money to make it happen—and life was a lot easier that way.

'Aren't you headed to Europe next week?' Sonny pushed on, not taking the hint. 'Why not look this girl up and see how she's doing?'

Coop stared blankly at his friend. He'd thought about it; of course he had. He had a meeting with some financiers in St Tropez who wanted to talk about franchising options for Dive Guys in the Med. It was only a short hop from there to London, where Ella lived. But…

'I don't know. if I went all the way out to London just to hook up, she might get the wrong idea.' He sure as hell didn't want Ella thinking this was more than it was.

'Why would that be bad?' Sonny's rueful smile made Coop feel about as smart as the lug nut he'd been trying to shift all morning. 'If she's the woman of your dreams.'

'Damn, Sonny, Ella is not the woman of my dreams,' he shot back, getting exasperated.

What was with Sonny? Was all this wedding garbage messing with his head and making him even more of a romantic than usual?

He hardly knew Ella. And he didn't have dreams about women. Well, not apart from R-rated ones. For the simple reason that he was more than happy being an island.

'If you say so.' Sonny shrugged, undaunted. 'But my point is you need to go get your sunshine back.' Sonny jerked his thumb over his shoulder, indicating the glimmering turquoise water that stretched towards the horizon. 'And if it's across that ocean that's where you oughta be.' His smile thinned. 'Because until you do, you're not a heck of a lot fun for anyone to be around.'

Coop frowned as he finally got the message. So that was it. Sonny wanted him out of the way while him and his family geared up for Josie's big day.

He felt the sharp stab of hurt. But guessed the old guy had a point. He had been pretty grouchy the last couple of months. Sleepless nights and sexual frustration could do that to a guy. And whatever was going on between him and Ella, it didn't seem to be getting any better. 'Have I really been that bad?' he asked.

Resting a solid hand on his shoulder, Sonny gave it a fatherly pat. 'Boy, you've been bitchier than when you were working all hours to set up your business.'

'Sorry.'

Sonny squeezed his shoulder. 'Don't be sorry, man, go do something about it.'

Coop nodded. What the hell? Trying to talk some sense into Josie and her folks about the wedding was a lost cause. And he could do with more than the two-day break he'd planned for his trip to the Med. Why not book a flight that routed through London? Stop over for a few extra days, book a suite in a classy hotel, see the city, and if he happened to be in Ella's neighbourhood at some point, why not look her up? If she wanted to throw some more sunshine his way—and maybe give him an explanation as to why she hadn't stuck around to say goodbye—why should he object?

As Sonny had said, he'd never had a woman walk out on him before now. That was most probably all this was really about. And if that made him an arrogant jackass, so be it. He needed to do something to get himself the hell over this hump he seemed to have got hung up on. So he could come back to Bermuda ready to smile through his teeth during his best friend's daughter's wedding.

What was the worst that could happen?

'Stop eating the merchandise! I don't care if you've got a cookie craving.'

Ella hastily wiped the white chocolate and macadamia nut evidence off her mouth. 'Sorry, I can't help it.'

Ruby sent her a superior look from the cappuccino machine, where she was busy whipping up a storm of decaf lattes and skinny mochas for the tennis foursome who had just arrived after a grudge match at the heath.

'You should be sorry. I'd love to know how you've barely gained an ounce.' Her gaze dipped to Ella's cleavage, displayed in the new D half-cup bra she'd splashed out on the previous week. 'Except on the bust.' Her eyes narrowed. 'Despite having consumed your own weight in confectionery in the last week.'

Ella grinned as she arranged the freshly baked passion-fruit florentines on the 'treat of the day' display. 'I'm simply making up for lost time. I could barely keep anything down for three solid weeks.'

Ella stroked the compact bulge that made the waistband of her hip-hugger jeans dig into her tummy. Even though she could not have been more ecstatic about the pregnancy, revelling in every change it brought to her body, puking her guts up every morning had got old fairly fast. And running a cake shop, where the cloying aroma of sweetness and the bitter chicory scent of coffee had been hell on her hypersensitive sense of smell, had been a particular brand of torture she had been more than happy to see the back of. Now she could simply enjoy all the other changes—well, all except one.

Her sex drive seemed to have mushroomed at the same pace as her bosom—if the lurid dreams she had most nights, in which a certain Cooper Delaney was a key player, were anything to go by.

Only last night, she'd woken up in a pool of sweat, her skin tight and oversensitive, her already enlarged nipples swollen and her engorged clitoris pulsing with the need to be touched. She'd never been all that self-sufficient, sexually speaking, before she'd met Cooper, but she'd had to take matters into her own hands more than once in the last few weeks, while visualising Cooper's honed, ripped body driving into her and hearing his deep laconic voice growling 'touch yourself' in her ear.

Heat boiled in her cheeks, at the memory of last night's frenzied and sadly dissatisfying orgasm. And the guilt that had followed. Was it possible that her body was playing tricks on her, constantly bringing up these carnal memories of her child's father to push her into contacting him the way she'd planned to do weeks ago?

But that was before she'd done an Internet search on him. And a simple investigation to discover his contact details had brought the panic seeping back.

Because putting Cooper Delaney's name and the words 'Bermuda' and 'snorkelling' into the search engine had brought up ten whole pages of references, not just to him but to Dive Guys, the phenomenally successful franchise he owned and operated in most of the Caribbean. A company that had been listed on the New York stock exchange for over three years and was—according to an article in *Time Life* magazine—one of the fastest-growing start-ups in the region.

She'd been in shock. Then she'd been upset that he hadn't trusted her enough to tell her the truth about himself... Then she'd thought of the secret child in her womb and she'd begun shaking so hard she'd had to lie down.

Coop Delaney wasn't a part-time boat captain and all around beach bum living a free-spirited, laid-back, itinerant existence on a Bermuda beach—he was an exceptionally rich and well-connected businessman with the money and influence to buy and sell her and Ruby's little cupcake bakery several hundred times over.

How could she tell a man like that she was carrying his child? And not expect him to make demands? Demands she might not want to agree to? If he'd been the Coop she'd thought he was, she would have phoned him weeks ago. But now...

'Check out the suit in the window.' Ruby's appreciative whistle woke Ella from her stupor. 'That guy's got
shoulders even a happily married woman can appreciate.'

Ella's gaze skimmed the top of the cookie display to
see a tall man, with closely cropped hair step into the café.
Recognition tickled her spine, then thumped into her chest
as he lifted his head and shockingly familiar emerald eyes
locked on hers.

She blinked rapidly, sure this had to be an apparition
conjured up by her guilty conscience—but then his sensual
lips quirked and the warm spot between her legs ignited.

'Hi, welcome to Touch of Frosting, Camden's premiere
cupcake bakery. What's your guilty pleasure this morning?'

Ella vaguely processed Ruby's familiar greeting through
the chainsaw in her head. 'Coop?' The word came out on
a rasp of breath.

'Hey there, Ella.' The apparition winked, which had
heat flushing to her hairline, before it addressed Ruby.
'You must be Ruby. The name's Coop. I'm a friend of
Ella's.'

He held out a deeply tanned hand in greeting as Ella
heard Ruby's sharp intake of breath.

'Hi.' Ruby skirted the counter and grasped his hand in
both of hers. 'Cooper Delaney, right? It's so fabulous to
actually meet you.'

Ella heard the perk of excitement in Ruby's voice and
the laconic ease in Coop's—and everything inside her
knotted with panic.

'Ella told you about me, huh?' His voice rumbled with
pleasure as the green gaze settled on her.

Say something.

Her mind screamed as she absorbed the chiselled perfection of his cheekbones, the tawny brows, the twinkle
of amusement in those arresting eyes, and the full sensual

lips that tilted up in a confidential smile. Arousal gripped her abdomen as blood pumped into her sex.

But then she noted all the things about this man that didn't fit: the slate-grey single-breasted suit, the clean-shaven jaw, the short, perfectly styled hair that was several shades darker with fewer strands of sun-streaked blond.

She shook her head, a bolt of raw panic slamming into her chest as he passed his palm in front of her face. He was speaking to her.

'Hey there, Ella, snap out of it. How you doing?'

I'm pregnant. And I should have got in touch with you weeks ago to tell you.

She opened parched lips, but couldn't force the words out.

'Ella's great, she had her first—' Ruby began.

'Shut up, Ruby!' The high-pitched squeal shot past the boulder lodged in her throat. Ruby's eyebrows rose to her hairline but thankfully she obeyed the command, while Coop's grin took on a curious tilt.

Ella skidded round the counter, galvanised out of her trance.

Get him out of here, then you can tell him. Sensibly, succinctly, and privately, without an audience of tennis players, yummy mummies, two giggling schoolgirls and your super-nosey best friend.

She owed him that much.

'I'm taking a half-day, Rubes.'

Ruby's brow furrowed.

Oh, dear, she'd have some explaining to do to Ruby, too. But that could wait, she thought, as she came to a halt in front of Cooper.

She tilted her head back, the effect of that lazy smile shimmering down to her toes. How could she have forgotten how tall he was? Taking a deep breath in, she got a lungful of his delicious scent.

He smells the same. Hold that thought.

But then the aroma of spicy cologne and soap and man triggered a renewed pulse of heat and the shudder of reaction hit her knees.

She grasped his arm, as much to stay upright as to propel him back out of the door before Ruby spilled any more confidential information. The bulge of muscle flexed beneath the soft fabric of his designer suit—which didn't do much for her leg tremors.

He glanced at her fingers and grinned, pleased with her haste. 'It's great to see you too, Ella.' That he didn't seem particularly fazed by her fruitcake behaviour helped to calm some of the tension screaming across her shoulder blades. 'I was just in the neighbourhood,' he added. 'And I figured we could catch up over....'

'That's wonderful, Coop,' she interrupted. 'But let's go somewhere private so we can talk properly.'

'Sounds good.' His hooded gaze suggested he had made a few assumptions about her eagerness to get him alone. And talking was not at the top of his current to-do list.

The stupid tingles raced across her skin.

Do not hold that thought. You need to keep a clear head.

She crossed to the door, still clinging onto his arm, but stopped in her tracks when he didn't move with her.

She swung back, ready to beg. 'Please, my flat's just round the corner. I have coffee. And cupcakes.'

Her gaze flicked over his shoulder to Ruby, who had crossed her arms over her chest and was staring at her, the concern on her face making Ella feel small and foolish.

'Cupcakes, huh?' He laughed, but then his hands cupped her elbows, forcing her to relinquish her death grip on his arm. 'I'm a sucker for cupcakes,' he purred, then yanked her onto tiptoes. 'But first things first.' He dipped his head, bringing his lips tantalisingly close. 'Don't I rate a "welcome to London" kiss?'

Before she had a chance to confirm or deny, his mouth settled over hers, and every thought bar one melted out of her head.

Yes, please.

His tongue coaxed her lips open in hungry strokes, then tangled with hers. The shaking in her legs shot off the Richter Scale but his arms wrapped around her waist, holding her steady against the lean, hard line of his body. His scent enveloped her, clogging her lungs as she clung to him for balance, and drank in the glorious urgency of his kiss.

As they broke apart she heard the smattering of applause from the group of mums in the corner. The heat rose up to scald her scalp—but he was smiling at her with that appreciative, sexy twist of his lips she remembered so well from Bermuda and she swallowed down the renewed bolt of panic.

She had so much to tell him, and she still had no real clue how he would respond. But kissing him again, having his arms around her, had felt so good, she refused to allow her doubts to resurface. She was having this beautiful man's baby—and it felt like fate somehow that he had come to London to see her.

He dropped his arms and slid one warm palm into hers. 'Let's get out of here.' He brushed his lips across her ear lobe. 'I'm dying to taste your cupcakes.'

She grinned, sure her cupcakes weren't the only thing he planned to taste. 'You're going to love them.'

She waved goodbye to Ruby, who sent her a wary smile back, then mouthed, 'Tell him.'

She nodded, sobering a little.

'Great to meet you, Ruby. I'll bring her back in one piece. I swear.' He sent Ruby a farewell salute as he opened the café door for her and she stepped outside. The sky was dark and overcast, a summer storm brewing, but excitement rippled.

Against all the odds, Cooper Delaney was here. And she would get the chance to tell him her news face to face. Now the initial shock had faded, she knew it was the best possible scenario. She could prepare him properly, before she told him. Explain exactly how it had happened and how much it meant to her, and make sure he understood he didn't have to be a part of the life growing inside her if he didn't want to be. That he had no obligations.

But surely him turning up here had to be a sign. Of something good. He'd come all this way to see her, and he'd kissed her with such fervour. The chemistry between them was still so strong, so hot. And there had been definite affection in his gaze too, the way his hands had steadied her, held her close.

He hadn't forgotten her, any more than she had forgotten him.

He slung an arm across her shoulders. 'Lead the way, my little cougar. But put a fire under it,' he said, casting a wary glance at the ominous thunderclouds overhead. 'It looks like we're about to get soaked.'

She chuckled, giddy with anticipation and tenderness, as a fat drop of rain landed on her cheek. 'My road is the second on the left.' The crash of thunder startled her for a moment, then the deluge of fat drops multiplied into a flood, drenching her T-shirt and jeans in seconds.

Laughing, she darted out from under his arm, the chilly summer rain plastering her hair against her cheeks and running in rivulets between her breasts. 'Come on, toy boy. I'll race you there,' she said, before sprinting off in a burst of energy.

They would work this out. Nothing bad could happen today. She was sure of it.

* * *

'Come back here…'

Cooper raced up the shadowy stairwell guided by that pert ass outlined in wet denim, his own shirt sticking to his chest.

He tripped, cursed, then finally caught up with her, his crotch throbbing now. Running with a hard-on was never a good idea, but he'd been waiting months to get his hands on her again.

Her light, infectious laugh bubbled through his blood, doing weird things to his equilibrium as he followed her into the shoebox apartment at the top of the stairs. He slammed the door behind him, taking in the compact living room, the kitchen counter, the couch covered in colourful cushions. Then grabbed a hold of one hundred pounds of wiggling, giggling female, and refused to let go.

'Got you.' He held her close, taking the time to study the open, heart-shaped face, the huge blue eyes that had haunted his dreams for weeks.

Maybe he had missed her, more than he thought.

'And you're not getting away from me any time soon,' he declared. Although she wasn't exactly trying too hard.

His lips captured hers in a hungry kiss, while he peeled off the drenched cotton T-shirt to discover the damp lemon-scented female flesh beneath.

He cupped her generous breasts, the pebbled nipples digging into his palms through her bra, then pinched the swollen tips, while his mouth drank in her soft grunts of excitement.

Her fingers threaded into his hair, tugging him back. 'I have to tell you…' Her voice came out on a whisper. 'We have to talk.'

'Later.' He nipped her bottom lip. 'Sex first. Then cupcakes. Talk after that.'

He delved to find the hook on her bra and sent up a silent prayer of thanks as it popped open. Dragging the wet hem of her T over her head, he ripped off the sodden bra.

When she was bare to the waist, her breasts heaved with her staggered breathing, the large reddened nipples like ripe berries, sweet and succulent.

'Those are even hotter than I remember.' He lifted his gaze, saw the flush of colour on high cheekbones, the blue of her eyes dilated to dark, driving need.

Cupping one heavy orb in his palm, he licked round the peak, heard her moan, then bit tenderly into the swollen tip, his erection now huge in his pants.

Her back arched as she thrust into his mouth, moaning softly as he suckled harder.

Finding the zipper of her jeans, he yanked down the tab, and delved beneath the clinging, constricting fabric to cup her. She sobbed as his fingers widened the slick folds, and touched the heart of her. She bucked, then grasped his wrist.

'Stop!' she cried. 'I'm going to come.'

'That's the general idea.' Panic clawed at his chest. If she said no now he was liable to die.

She stared at him, her need plain in the wide pupils, the staggered pants of breath. 'I want you inside me. It's been too long.'

'Not a problem.' He chuckled, relief flooding through him as the tension in his groin begged for release. 'Then let's get naked. Fast.'

The sound of frantic cursing, of tearing fabric, of buttons hitting the linoleum flooring filled the small room as they wrestled to get their wet clothes off as fast as humanly possible.

After what felt like several millennia she stood naked before him, her gaze darkening further as those bright eyes dropped to his groin. His erection twitched, the pulse throbbing at its tip, steady and relentless.

He lifted her against the wall of the apartment, wedging himself into the space between her thighs. Clasping her generous hips, he assessed those spectacular breasts. She'd gained some weight since their night in Bermuda and it suited her—the belly that had been so flat across her hip bones now pillowing his erection.

The dumb wave of regret that her body had undergone that small change and he hadn't been there to see it, to witness it, passed over like a shadow then disappeared as her breasts pressed into his chest—demanding more friction. He ducked his head, to suck at the pulse point in her neck, which beat in frantic flutters. Her addictive scent surrounded him, lemon and spice and all things nice.

His lips curved, holding her as she hooked toned legs around his waist. Her fingers threaded into the short, damp hair at his ears.

'I haven't got any condoms,' he admitted, his mind trying to engage with the need to slow the hell down. To think through the driving urge to sink into her tight heat. He hadn't had time to stop and pick any protection up because he'd come straight from the airport. And he hadn't figured things would get this hot, this quickly. But could he risk it? Just this once? She was on the pill? 'You okay with me using withdrawal? I'm clean, I swear.'

He felt her nod, and lifted his head to see her eyes, glazed with an emotion that made his heart thud against his chest wall like a sledgehammer.

'So am I,' she replied

It was all the permission he needed. His shaft jerked against her belly from the kick of desperation. Palming her buttocks, and angling her pelvis as best he could, he thrust home in one long, solid glide. Her slick, wet sex stretched to receive him, then massaged him like a velvet vice. Her head dropped back, thudding the wall, as he began to move, the thrusts jerky, desperate, the need quickly becoming too fast and furious, the need so raw and draining he couldn't slow down, couldn't stop now if his life depended on it.

She sobbed, her fingernails scraping his back as she clung on. Her muscles began to milk him, and he knew she was coming.

Don't pull out. Not yet. Hold on. Damn it.

His seed boiled, driving up from his balls, hurling him closer and closer to the cliff edge, her sobs of completion beckoning him to come faster, harder. And a tiny part of his mind screamed to the animal inside him.

Now. Pull out, now.

He wrenched himself free. Dropping his head against her shoulder, kissing the salt, sweet taste of her neck, the pain of separation as devastating as the brutal, unstoppable roll of orgasm as his seed pumped into the welcoming softness of her belly.

'Damn, that was even more awesome than I remember.'

Ella's gaze shimmered back into focus as a rough palm touched her cheek and blunt fingers sank into her hair. Those deep emerald eyes searched her face, making her chest tighten.

She nodded, gently, feeling stunned, her sex still clenching and releasing from the intensity of her orgasm. Seemed absence didn't just make the heart grow fonder.

'Yes,' she whispered, her throat raw from the wellspring of emotion.

His lips curved, and he placed a tender kiss on her forehead. 'Come on.' He hefted her into his arms, bracing his forearm under her buttocks as she held onto his shoulders. 'Let's grab a shower. Then I want a cupcake.'

'But we still need to talk,' she murmured against his neck.

'Sure. But first I want to see that magnificent rack covered in soap suds.'

She chuckled, resting her head on his shoulder, and draping her arms around his neck, her emotions too close to the surface to protest. Surely a few more minutes of intimacy, of getting reacquainted, wouldn't do any harm—she'd waited this long already?

Locating the tiny bathroom at the back of the flat, he put her down to twist on the shower. But kept one hand on her hip, as if he were afraid she'd run off. She remembered leaving him, that morning with only a thank you. And felt the renewed trickle of guilt.

The water gurgled and spurted out of the shower head, the stream thin and underwhelming.

'Is that as good as it gets?' he remarked.

She smiled. 'This is British plumbing we're talking about. That's the equivalent of Niagara Falls.'

His quick grin lifted her spirits and made the trickle of guilt dry up.

'At least it's hot,' he said, testing the temperature before he hauled her into the cubicle.

'Not for long.'

He grabbed her lemon verbena soap off the ledge, and worked up a lather, his hair plastered to his head, his eyes wicked with intent. 'Then we better get this party started.'

Gentle hands cupped her breasts, lifting and testing the weight as his thumbs glided over pebbled nipples. The heat pulsed and tugged between her thighs.

She took the soap to wash him in return, putting all the emotion she felt into the task as her hands stroked the lean, muscular slopes of his abdomen, explored the roped sinews that defined his hip bones. She took his penis into her palm, felt it lengthen and harden as she caressed it.

Blood surged into her tender clitoris, and she knew she wanted him again, already, surging deep, the delicious decadent stretching feeling of his flesh entering hers. Touching her womb where their child grew.

Soon he would know, and, whatever his reaction, surely it would be okay, when this closeness, this physical joining felt so good, so right.

But then he lifted her breasts, the cooling water sluicing away the soap, and said, 'I like the extra weight—it looks great on you.'

The approval in his gaze had the wave of guilt flopping over in her stomach. She couldn't wait any longer. It wasn't fair to him, or to their child. She drew away from him, her back wedged against the wall of the cubicle.

'We need to get dressed. I have something I have to tell you.'

'Okay.'

He flipped off the shower control, but took hold of her wrist as she opened the cubicle door. The sudden silence felt deafening, despite the blood roaring in her ears. He tugged her towards him as he stepped out behind her, tucked a finger under her chin, lifting her gaze to his. 'What's up? Is something wrong?'

'No, I just…' She gulped past the tightness.

Not yet. Get yourself together first. You need to tell him gently. Carefully.

Her gaze dropped to his erection. She certainly couldn't function, let alone think clearly, while he was standing naked in front of her, visibly aroused.

'I just need a minute.'

His grip had loosened, his gaze puzzled, but not yet wary. She pulled her hand free, headed for the door. 'Shall we get dressed? I can meet you in the living room in ten minutes? Make you that coffee I promised?'

He shrugged, grabbed a towel from the rail to wrap around his waist. 'Sure.'

She darted out of the door before he could change his mind.

* * *

'All right, let's have it, what was so important we couldn't finish what I was busy starting in the shower?'

Ella smiled at the rueful tone, and glanced up from the cupcakes she was busy arranging on a plate.

He stood with his legs crossed at the ankles, leaning against the kitchen counter. He'd changed into a pair of faded jeans and a black T-shirt, which must have been in the bag he'd had with him. Had he come straight from the airport, then, to see her? She felt a renewed spike of optimism, of hope.

She'd figured so many outcomes for what she was about to tell him, but none of them had included the possibility that he might be pleased with her news. Yes, it would be a shock, but why had she assumed it would necessarily be a disaster?

She never would have guessed he would come to London, or the chemistry between them would have remained as hot for him as it still was for her.

'Why don't you sit down?' She gestured towards the living area. 'The coffee will be ready any minute.'

His brows lifted, the rueful grin taking on a mischievous tilt. 'It's not coffee I want.' Stepping close to hold her chin, he gave her lips a quick peck. The kiss felt casual and affectionate. The hope swelled in her chest. 'But we'll play it your way, for now.'

He settled on the sofa, while she fussed over the coffee for another precious few minutes, getting her thoughts lined up.

Finally she couldn't put it off any longer. Sitting on the opposite sofa, she placed the plate of cherry-chocolate cupcakes on the coffee table and poured him a cup of coffee. She had a momentary wobble when he told her he took it black, and it occurred to her how much she didn't know about him.

Don't chicken out now. Telling him is the first step to finding out all those things you don't know.

She took a long fortifying sip of the fennel tea she'd made for herself. 'I'm not sure where to start,' she began, galvanised by the thought that she was excited about taking this new step.

He lifted a cupcake off the plate. 'Then why don't you start by telling me why you ran out on me?'

'I didn't,' she said, frowning at the slight edge in his voice. 'I woke up and you were gone. I figured you'd run out on me.'

'Damn, seriously?' He looked genuinely stunned, which was a balm to her ego.

'Well, yes. And I felt uncomfortable with your friend Josie there.' She remembered the spike of dismay and asked, 'Who is she, by the way? She seemed to know you exceptionally well.'

His eyebrows rose and his lips crinkled. 'Are you jealous?'

Colour stained her cheeks.

He chuckled. 'Josie's like a kid sister. An annoying kid sister. Believe me, you've got nothing to be jealous of.'

'I didn't say I was jealous.'

'Uh-huh.' He sent her a confident smile. And she huffed out a laugh. The tension in her chest easing.

He took a large bite of the cupcake, held it up. 'Damn, that's good.' Finishing it off in a few quick bites, he placed the paper casing on the plate. 'So why don't you spill it, whatever it is you have to talk about. Before we get back into the shower.'

The colour in her cheeks flared again, under his watchful gaze. 'Okay, it's, well, it's sort of hard to say right out.'

She gulped down the new lump in her throat.

'Yeah? That doesn't sound good.' He sent her a crooked

smile. 'I really hope you're not going to tell me you're married.'

She laughed, the tension dissolving a little. 'God, no, it's nothing like that. It's...' She examined her fingers, suddenly shy rather than scared. Wouldn't it be amazing if he was actually as excited about this as she was? 'Actually, I'm pregnant. That's why, well, I've gained some weight.'

The crooked smile remained, but the curiosity in his eyes turned to astonishment as his gaze dipped to her breasts and then her belly. He straightened on the sofa, his mouth opening. Then closing. Then opening again. 'You...? You're expecting a kid? You don't look pregnant.'

She waited for the obvious next question, but he just continued to stare at her belly.

'Well, I'm only twelve weeks, so it doesn't show much yet.' She placed her hands on the slight swelling, suddenly keen to emphasise it for his benefit.

His head lifted. She'd expected surprise, even shock when he made the connection; she'd even prepared herself for annoyance, and anger. What she hadn't prepared herself for, though, was the way the relaxed, sexy charm had been ripped away to be replaced by complete horror. 'Tell me you're not saying what I think you're saying?'

Her pulse throbbed painfully in her neck, and she cradled her abdomen, the urge to shield her child, instinctive. She couldn't speak, so she simply nodded.

He leapt up from the sofa like a puppet who had been rudely jerked on stage. The vicious swear word echoed around the tiny room. 'You have got to be kidding me? It can't be mine—you said you were on the pill.'

She'd expected this accusation, on the numerous occasions when she'd had this conversation in her head. But all the careful explanations, the reasoned arguments, the excuses absolving her all seemed to pale into insignificance in the face of his frantic denial. And all she could manage was, 'I know, I realised when I found out you may have got that impression, but I—'

'You lied to me?' He stepped forward, the stance threatening.

Somehow she knew he wouldn't hurt her, not physically, but she could see the turmoil of emotion and it made her insides tangle into tight, torturous knots, the guilt that she'd kept so carefully at bay for weeks creating a yawning chasm in the pit of her stomach.

'Why the hell did you lie?' He dug his fingers into his hair, sending the damp strands into deep furrows. 'Unless… Hell… You wanted to get knocked up? Is this a setup? You figure I'll pay you off?'

The accusation came so far out of left-field, she hadn't seen it coming before it had smacked into her chest and hurled her heart into her throat. 'What? No. I never…' Her denial choked off at the contempt in his eyes. 'You used a condom—how could I have planned it?'

'I knew the cute and clueless act was too good to be true. But I fell for it anyway.'

'What act? What are you talking about?'

'Drop it, okay. You've got what you wanted.' His eyes slid back to her belly, the light in them harsh and resentful. 'My bun in your oven.'

'No, you don't understand. It was never planned.' The justification, the explanation at last came tumbling out. 'The pregnancy was…is an accident. It was all so rushed and…I didn't think it would matter that I wasn't on the pill.'

'You didn't think it would matter?' His voice rose to a shout. 'Are you nuts? I told you I didn't want to risk it. What the hell about that did you not understand?'

'No, that's not what I meant. I didn't think I could….' She faltered, unable to reveal the truth about her medical history, her fertility issues, the test results she'd gone to

Bermuda to escape. She couldn't tell this stranger about any of that; it would make her too vulnerable, too raw, especially now, with her throat already aching with unshed tears.

'You don't have to be involved.' She scrambled to justify, to explain, to avert the terrible feeling of loss. 'I've made the decision to have this child. I want it. Very much.' Her hands shook, the trembling having moved up from her toes, to her knees and across her torso.

Don't you dare cry.

Why hadn't she said all of this to start with, before she'd told him about the pregnancy? He obviously thought she was some kind of gold-digger. If she could just make him understand he didn't have to feel responsible for this child, everything would be okay. But even as she told herself it, a part of her was dying inside at the knowledge that Cooper Delaney hated her now.

'I just thought you should know.'

'Right, so now I know,' he snarled. 'Thanks for that. And what the hell am I supposed to do with the information? You've told me a part of me is going to be walking around on this planet and I don't get to have any say in that?'

She shook her head, the tears drying up inside her. *Stay firm. Stay strong. Don't break, not this time.* 'No. No, you don't.' She firmed her lips to stop them trembling. 'I won't have an abortion. And nothing you can do or say will make me.'

He flinched. 'Who said anything about an abortion?'

'I won't do it. I want this baby very much. If you don't, that's okay. You never have to have anything to do with it.'

'Yeah, right.' Marching past her, he grabbed his bag off the floor. 'Like that's going to work.' He slung the leather holdall over his shoulder and opened the door. Rain slashed down in angry currents against the hall window. But the summer storm that had seemed so cleansing, so perfect, so passionate only hours before, now appeared grey and dark and oppressive.

He sent her one last scathing look over his shoulder, the look of betrayal in his eyes palpable. And then slammed the door behind him.

She sank down against the wall, her legs too shaky to hold her, and pressed her forehead into her knees. And listened to his footfalls, heavy on the stairs, fade away into nothingness.

Coop stumbled out onto the street, his heart hitting his ribcage hard enough to shatter bone. Rain slashed at his face as he dumped his bag on the sidewalk and smashed his fist into the brick wall that marked the perimeter of her apartment building.

Pain hurtled up his arm, lanced across his knuckles, but went some way to dulling the terrifying emotions consuming him.

You dumbass. What the hell were you thinking? Coming here? Trusting her?

He sucked the battered knuckles, and picked up his bag in the other hand.

He hailed a cab, jumped in out of the rain and shouted through the grill, 'Take me to a hotel.'

'How about the Renaissance, sir? It's pricey but very plush.'

'Sure, great, whatever,' he croaked, his voice hoarse, his whole body starting to shake. He didn't give a damn where he went—he just had to get away from the memory of those big eyes glossy with unshed tears.

But then he caught the glittering pink logo on the window of Ella's cupcake store as the cab sped past it. The panic boiled in his gut as the taste of her lingered on his tongue and the residual heat throbbed in his crotch. Mocking him.

He sank his head into his hands and wanted to howl with pain and frustration.

God help him, it didn't matter what he did now, or how much money he made or how fast he ran—he could never ever be an island again. And it was all his own damn fault.

CHAPTER EIGHT

COOP STARED AT the glittery pink lettering on the front of the diner, and then past it through the glass. He spotted Ella in front of the counter, busy chatting to a customer, her hand resting casually on her belly—and swallowed to ease the thickening in his throat.

Play it cool. No more freak-outs allowed.

He'd spent a night in the gothic splendor of the five-star hotel overlooking St Pancras Station, not sleeping a wink, as he went over every single thing she'd said, and every single thing he'd said. And he'd come to a few important—if shattering—conclusions.

He didn't have the first clue what he was supposed to do about the bomb she'd just exploded in his nice, easy, island life. Correction: his formerly nice, easy, island life. Fatherhood was something he hadn't planned for and didn't know a damn thing about.

And he hated not knowing, because it reminded him too much of his childhood. The dead weight of responsibility, the relentless pressure of being constantly trapped without a way out and that terrifying feeling of insecurity, of never knowing if he would be strong enough, smart enough, man enough to make things right for his mom.

He didn't want to live through all that again. And he hated that he would have to now.

And because of that he'd panicked yesterday, when Ella

had told him her news—and had dropped a pretty big bomb on her in return.

Because however much he might want to blame all this on Ella, he knew now—once he'd taken the time to examine all the facts—that he couldn't. He also knew he couldn't just walk away from his own kid and forget about it—the way she'd suggested—because that would make him no better than his old man. And he was pretty sure he couldn't do that and live with himself afterwards.

All of which left him with only one option. Suck it up, stop whining about what he couldn't change and try to deal with it.

And the only way he could do that was to deal with Ella first.

Forcing the trademark 'never-let-them-see-you're-scared' smile he'd perfected as a kid onto his lips, he pushed open the door. But as Ella's gaze locked on his and her eyes went wide with distress his step faltered, his heartbeat stumbled and the thickening in his throat got a hell of a lot worse.

'Coop?' Ella bit into her lip, the tremor of shock and anxiety almost as overwhelming as the wave of relief.

She'd never expected to see him again, had convinced herself that his angry departure was for the best. She'd told herself over and over again during a long night spent on the phone to Ruby, and then lying in bed staring at the crack in her ceiling, that she couldn't make Coop want to be a father—any more than she could make him forgive her for something she hadn't done. So it would be pointless and futile to contact him again.

'We need to talk,' he said, his deep voice slightly strained but with none of the explosive anger from their last encounter. 'Can you take a break?'

She nodded, too stunned to speak, then glanced round

the shop to locate her business partner. Ruby stood chatting to a young couple to whom she'd just delivered a couple of chai lattes. But then her head came up and she spotted Coop. All traces of the genial hostess disappeared as she marched back across the café.

'What do you want?' Ruby stepped behind the counter to stand shoulder to shoulder with Ella. 'Haven't you done enough?'

'I'm here to talk to Ella, honey, not you,' Coop said, the casual tone in direct contrast to the challenge in his eyes.

'Well, "honey"…' Ruby sneered the endearment, squaring up for a fight '…you're going to have to go through me to get to her after the immature way you behaved yesterday.'

'It's okay, Ruby.' Ella touched her friend's arm, emboldened by her support—even if it was counterproductive right now.

The last thing she wanted was for Coop to find out how much his accusations had hurt her, or how she'd dissolved into a quivering wreck after his departure. Showing that kind of weakness would only put her on the defensive. 'Coop's right—we need to talk. Is it okay if I take a few minutes?'

'Are you sure?' Ruby asked.

'We'll need more than a few minutes to sort this mess out,' Coop interrupted before she could reassure her friend. 'I've got a car waiting outside to take us back to my hotel, so we can have some privacy.'

This mess.

Ella's heart shrank. Her baby wasn't a mess. But if that was the way Coop saw it, then sorting out his involvement—or rather the lack of it—would be fairly clear cut. And she supposed she should be glad that he seemed prepared to do that much.

'Why do you need privacy?' Ruby interrupted again.

'So you can shag her and then have another temper tantrum like a two-year—'

'Ruby, please, don't.' Ella raised her voice, grateful for the spark of indignation. 'I'll be fine. All we're going to do is talk.' She wasn't about to make the mistake again of believing the strong physical attraction between them meant an emotional connection too.

She really didn't know this man. His volatile reaction last night had proved that. This 'talk' would be a chance to find out more about him—while also reassuring him that her expectations of him were zero as far as the baby was concerned.

Ruby continued to eyeball Coop for several pregnant seconds, but, instead of rising to the provocation, he grinned.

'You heard the lady.' He slung his hands in his pockets, the picture of nonchalance as he raised an eyebrow, the challenge unmistakable. 'All we're going to do is talk.' His gaze landed on Ella and the unwanted hum of awareness seared through her body. 'This time.'

'How are you? Is everything okay with the kid?'

Ella turned, to find Coop watching her from the opposite side of the cab as it crawled down Camden High Road. After persuading Ruby that she was woman enough to handle a private chat with her baby's father, she'd been careful to seat herself as far away as possible from him. But the tentative enquiry and the flicker of concern knocked her off balance again.

'Yes, everything's good.'

'I just wondered because…' he paused to clear his throat, looking more uncomfortable than she'd ever seen him '…I was kind of rough with you. In your apartment. You know, before you told me.'

She blinked, puzzled. He hadn't been rough, not until

after he'd heard the news and then only verbally. But then it dawned on her what he was referring to. Their frantic lovemaking against the wall. The blush climbed into her cheeks and heat pulsed in her sex at the visceral memory. While a matching, much more dangerous warmth tugged under her breastbone.

'Oh, no, everything's fine, really. Sex isn't a problem in pregnancy—as long as we don't start breaking furniture it should be okay.' The blush launched up to her hairline as it occurred to her what she had implied. 'Not that we're likely to be…well, you know.'

The sensual smile was even more unsettling. 'Yeah, I get it.' He tapped his fingers against his knee. 'Listen, I owe you another apology.'

She struggled not to be seduced by the smouldering look he appeared to be sending her, which she decided had to be an optical illusion. After their argument yesterday, he wasn't likely to jump her again. And she definitely did not plan to jump him.

'What for?' she said, unable to deny the tiny trickle of hope at his conciliatory tone. The less acrimony between them, the more chance they had of making this talk as painless as possible.

'For losing my temper. For freaking out when you told me…' his gaze dipped pointedly to her belly '…about your condition. For making out like this was all your fault.'

Relief was sharp and sweet at the heartfelt words. 'So you don't believe I got pregnant to set you up any more?'

He had the grace to look embarrassed. 'Not once I'd examined the facts. I figure opening that first condom packet with my teeth probably wasn't the smartest thing I've ever done.' His gaze fixed on her. 'And after what happened yesterday, I'm guessing even if you had told me the truth about being on the pill, I would have risked it. Things had got pretty hot by then already.'

The muscles of her thighs melted as the pesky hum of reaction shimmered down to her core.

'I appreciate your honesty.' She nodded, accepting his apology with deliberate formality, while crossing her legs in an attempt to ease the ache in her sex.

Not going there. Remember?

'I owe you an apology, too.' She heaved a sigh, knowing she was hardly blameless in the misunderstandings that had arisen between them.

'Yeah?' He arched a questioning brow.

'I should have corrected you…' The blush fired up her neck as his lips quirked, the sensual knowledge in his smile not doing a thing to cool the hot spot between her thighs. 'But I wasn't really paying a lot of attention to the conversation at that point.'

'You and me both.' The low comment was husky with intimacy.

She cleared her throat. *Hormones behave. Now.* 'But to be honest, I really didn't think it would make any difference because…' She hesitated. 'I've had some fertility issues. Believe me, the chances of me getting pregnant were extremely slim.'

He frowned. 'How slim?'

'Well, if my doctor's reaction is anything to go by when she confirmed the pregnancy, I think we might be talking lottery-winning odds.'

'Damn. Seriously?'

She nodded, smiling at his reaction. He sounded more stunned than pleased, but it still felt good to share such an important moment in their child's life with him.

'When did you find out?' he asked, and her smile faded. *Blast.*

'Um…' She glanced out of the window as the pristine new Eurostar terminal at St Pancras Station inched by.

'You know, that you were knocked up?' he prompted, obviously thinking she hadn't understood the question.

She studied the station's redbrick Victorian grandeur as they turned onto Euston road, desperate to avoid his unsettling gaze and the equally unsettling question. He'd been honest with her, and she knew she owed him the same courtesy, but would telling him the truth break this momentary truce? Obviously, she should have contacted him weeks ago, and she hadn't. If only she hadn't been such a coward.

'What's the deal, Ella?' he probed, already sounding suspicious. 'How long have you known about this?'

She sighed. 'Four weeks.'

She tensed at the muffled curse as the cab stopped outside the station hotel.

'Great.' He didn't say another word, just paid the cabbie and ushered her into the Renaissance's grand lobby area.

Every time she'd passed the historic hotel since its renovation a few years ago, she'd wondered what it looked like inside. But she barely registered the lavish vaulted ceiling or the plush interior design as his palm settled on the small of her back, and he directed her to the elevators.

His suite on the third floor had a spiral wrought-iron staircase that curved onto a second level, and original Gothic arched windows that looked down onto the station concourse. But as he poured out the bottle of sparkling mineral water she'd requested into a glass filled with ice it wasn't the hotel's palatial elegance she found intimidating.

'Okay, so now I want to know—why the delay?' He helped himself to a cola from the room's bar. 'Because I've got to tell you, I'm not feeling real happy about the fact that you've known about this kid for a month and you didn't get in touch.'

She'd been expecting the question ever since they'd arrived. And had prepared an answer. But she paused to take a hasty gulp of the icy, effervescent water.

She didn't want to tell him how she'd initially panicked about his reaction. Because then she'd have to tell him about Randall, and the child she'd lost. And she didn't see how that would serve any purpose now. Except to make her look bad. And she looked bad enough already.

'Stop stalling, Ella,' he murmured, watching her over the rim of his glass. And she had the disconcerting thought again that he seemed to be able to read her a lot easier than she was able to read him.

'All right,' she huffed, perching on a bar stool. 'If you must know, I did an internet search to get your details, so I could contact you.' This wasn't lying, she justified, it was simply failing to tell the whole truth. 'And, well...' Okay, maybe this part of the truth made her seem a little pathetic. But pathetic she could live with.

'And...?' he prompted, as if he didn't already know what she was going to say.

'I thought you were a freelance boat captain who lived in a one-room beach shack. I wasn't expecting to discover your name mentioned as one of the top young entrepreneurs in the Caribbean. It was disconcerting.'

He sent her an unapologetic smile.

What was so funny?

'And totally unexpected,' she added. 'I needed time to adjust to that before contacting you. So I waited, probably a bit longer than I should have.'

'A bit?' The grin spread as he propped himself on the bar stool next to her and nudged her knee with his. Crowding her personal space. 'Four weeks is an awful lot of adjustment time, don't you think? And you never did contact me, honey. I came to you.'

'There was an awful lot to adjust to.' She raised her chin. He'd tricked her, and pretended to be someone he wasn't. Surely she was entitled to be a little miffed about that? 'It made me realise that I didn't really know anything about you, and that scared me.'

'You knew the important stuff.' He ran his thumb across her bottom lip.

'Don't.' She jerked back, the sudden touch almost as shocking as the tenderness in his eyes.

'You scare pretty easy, don't you, Ella?' The probing gaze made her feel as if he could see through her T-shirt and jeans to the naked, needy girl she'd once been. 'Why is that?'

She tried to regulate her staggered breathing, unable to take her eyes off his.

Sexual desire was something she could handle. Would handle. But she didn't want to need him. To need any man. Not again.

'Do you think we could talk about the baby now?' she said. 'I have to get back to work.'

'Sure.' Coop shrugged, the tension in his shoulder blades nothing compared to the kick of need in his crotch.

Damn, he wanted her again: that lush mouth on his, those hard nipples grinding against his chest, the hot, wet heat gripping him like a velvet glove.

And he was pretty damn sure she wanted him too.

He could smell her arousal, the spicy scent of her need, ever since she'd climbed into the cab and sat stiffly in the far corner, as if she was worried she'd spontaneously combust if she got too close.

She still fascinated him, and excited him. And even though he kept telling himself hooking up with her again had the potential to turn this mess into a total disaster—another part of him was thinking this mess couldn't get much bigger if it tried. So why should they deny themselves? Only problem was, he wasn't sure if that part of him was the part that was supposed to be doing the thinking, or a part that was positioned a lot further south.

He had to admit he was also very curious, as well as kind of touched, by her reaction when she'd discovered the truth about Dive Guys and his wealth. Wouldn't most women feel entitled to hit him for some kind of compensation? Especially once they found out how much he was worth? Instead of that she'd 'needed time to adjust'? What was with that? One thing, it sure didn't make him feel any better about having accused her of setting him up.

He poured the last of his cola into his glass, took a long swig to buy himself some time and figure out what to do now.

She hadn't said anything, the expectation in her face tempered by wariness. As if she was worried about what he was going to say, but determined to put the best possible spin on it.

'The way I see it, Ella,' he began, acknowledging that it was definitely a strike in his favour that she was so easy to read, 'however this happened, we're both going to be parents of the same kid. And you're right, we don't know nearly enough about each other.' He let his eyes wander over her torso, vindicated by the bullet points thrusting against the tight cotton of her T. 'Except in the most basic sense.' He slugged down the last of the cola, and let the cool caffeinated liquid soothe his parched throat. 'How about you come back to Bermuda for a couple of weeks?' The offer came out of his mouth before he'd really had a chance to consider it, but it instantly felt right when her eyes lit up with delighted astonishment. 'And while you're there we can iron out how we're going to handle stuff once the kid's born.'

'You want to be involved? In the baby's life?' She sounded so overjoyed, he had to bite the inside of his mouth to keep from grinning back at her. Was it really going to be that easy?

'Of course I do. It's my kid too, isn't it?'

'Well, yes. Yes, it is.' She flattened her hands across her abdomen, in that protective gesture that he was beginning to realise was entirely instinctive. And totally genuine.

His heartbeat slowed at the evidence of how much the baby meant to her already, even though it was probably no bigger than a shrimp. Then fluttered uncomfortably, at the knowledge that his child was unlikely to ever mean that much to him.

He could do responsibility, and loyalty, and commitment, up to a point. But the kind of blind faith and trust you needed to care about someone more than you cared about yourself? Forget it. He knew he'd never be able to do that again.

'What on earth do you mean you're going to Bermuda?' Ruby stared. 'For how long?'

'I'm not sure, probably only a fortnight. He suggested I get an open ticket, but I doubt it'll take longer than that.' Although she had to admit she'd been impossibly touched when he'd sounded concerned that two weeks might not be enough time to sort out 'all the baby stuff'.

'Are you completely bonkers?' Ruby propped her hands on her hips, the belligerent stance one Ella recognised.

'He's invited me and I think it's a good idea.' She sprinkled edible pink glitter onto the swirl of buttercream icing. And placed the finished cupcake onto the tower she was assembling for a nine-year-old's birthday party, refusing to make eye contact with her friend. She'd expected this reaction. It didn't mean she was going to enjoy dealing with it. She hated arguing with Ruby. 'We're having a child together. I'd like him to be involved if he wants to be, but I need to know a lot more about him to make that a realistic possibility. Especially as we live so far apart.' She'd thought it all out, and it all made perfect sense.

Ruby tapped her foot. 'So why can't he stay in London so you can sort all that out here?'

Ella sighed, and wiped sugary hands on her apron. 'He has a business to run.'

'So do you.' Ruby went straight for the jugular.

'I know it's not a good time.' Ella faced her friend, and shook off the sting of guilt. They were already having to take out a loan to cover the extra staffing costs while she went on maternity leave, but... 'It will be good for Sally and Gemma to have a trial run with you supervising before I have the baby and I've got enough saved to cover the cost of their wages while I'm away.'

'You know very well this has nothing to do with the money,' Ruby pointed out. 'What about your antenatal appointments? What if something happens with the baby?'

'Coop's arranged for the top obstetrician on the island to handle my care while I'm there.' Even if he had gone a little pale when she'd mentioned the problem. 'But it's unlikely to be more than a couple of weeks. I'll still only be four months when I get back.'

'Fine, well, now for the biggie.' Ruby threw up her hands in exasperation. 'What about the fact that Cooper Delaney is a complete jerk who accused you of being a gold-digger, and a liar and had you in floods of tears less than twenty-four hours ago? How do you know you can trust him not to be a jerk again once you're stuck in Bermuda with him?'

I don't.

Ella pushed away the doubt. He'd lost the plot when she'd told him about the baby, but he'd apologised for that and she knew he meant it. And anyway, this really wasn't about her. 'He's the father of my child and he's giving me a chance to get to know him better. Surely you can see I have to take it?'

'Umm-hmm. And you don't find it the tiniest bit suspicious that twenty-four hours after totally flipping out about this pregnancy he suddenly wants to be so intimately involved in it...' Ruby paused for effect '...and you.'

'Maybe.' Of course she'd thought about it. After the initial euphoria at his offer, she'd calmed down enough to realise his sudden interest in the baby might not be the only reason he'd asked her to come to Bermuda.

But that didn't alter the fact that he was the father of her child. And she did want him to be involved. And that going to Bermuda was the only way to find out if they could make that happen.

'You're absolutely determined to do this, aren't you?' Ruby sounded pained.

'Yes.'

Ruby cursed sharply, defeated. 'I guess it's my own fault. If I hadn't interfered and encouraged you to nail Captain Studly in the first place, you wouldn't be in this situation.'

Ella grasped Ruby's cheeks, forcing her gaze back to hers. 'What situation? Getting the chance to have a child of my own? Getting to experience the miracle of becoming a mum? Something I was sure would never be possible? That situation?'

Ruby sent her a lopsided smile. 'Okay, point taken. But do me a favour, okay?'

'What favour?'

'Don't let all your happy over the pregnancy blind you to the truth about what's really going on with him. You have a tendency to always want to see the best in people, Ella. And that's one of the things I love about you. But try to be a little bit cautious this time.'

'If this is about what happened with Randall, you don't

have to worry.' Ella threaded her fingers through Ruby's and held on. 'I'm not going into this blind. I learnt that lesson when I was eighteen I'll never fall in love that easily again.' She'd made that mistake with Randall, and her baby had paid the price. 'But I refuse to go into this scared either.'

She needed to take some risks, to solve the fascinating enigma that was Cooper Delaney. A man who had the laid-back, laconic charm of a beach bum, but had the drive and ambition to build a multimillion-dollar empire from nothing. A man who could worry about the child growing in her womb when they made love, and yet look at her with a hunger that burned right down to her soul.

She wanted to understand him—to know how he really felt about this pregnancy and this baby and her—but only so he could play an active role in her child's life.

She wasn't looking for anything else. She was sure of it.

CHAPTER NINE

'HOW WAS THE TRIP?' Coop reached in to grab her suitcase
as Ella stepped out of the air-conditioned taxi into the shel-
tered carport rimmed by palm trees and flowering vines
at the back of his property.

She fanned her face with the wide-brimmed straw hat
she'd bought at the airport as the afternoon heat enveloped
her. Bermuda in April had been in the mid-seventies and
pleasantly hot; in late July it was hitting the high eighties
and seemed to be sucking the life-force right out of her
tired limbs.

'Good. Thank you.' She huffed to stop her sweaty hair
sticking to her forehead as Coop paid the driver and waved
him off.

The truth was it had been better than good, when she'd
arrived at Gatwick Airport to discover the economy class
ticket she'd insisted on purchasing herself, despite several
terse emails from Coop before she left London, had been
upgraded to first class. The added benefits of a three-
course cordon bleu meal and a fold-down bed had made
the eight-hour flight pass in a haze of anticipation. But now
she was here, the impact of seeing him again was making
the crows of doubt swoop like vultures in her stomach.

'I appreciated the upgrade, but you really didn't need
to do that.' She wanted to make it absolutely clear she did
not expect him to bankroll her.

Picking up her suitcase, he slung her carry-on bag under his arm. 'Sure I did.' His gaze skimmed down to her midriff before he sent her an assured grin. 'No baby of mine travels coach.'

The vultures in her stomach soared upward to flap around her heart and she stood like a dummy, stupidly touched by the reference to their child.

'Come here.' Resting his hand on her waist, he directed her towards the wooden steps that led out of the carport and into the back of the house. 'Let's get you out of this heat.'

The stairs led to the wide veranda of a white, wood-framed house that rose from the grove of palms to stand on a rocky outcropping. She'd admired the modern, two-storey colonial structure as they wound down the drive from the main gate. Up close, the building was dominated by the large windows covered by louvred shutters. The house appeared cool and airy even before they stepped off the veranda into a palatial, high-ceilinged living area that opened onto a wraparound porch, which looked down onto the cove below.

Dumping her bag and suitcase at the base of a curving staircase that led to the second level, Coop leaned against the balustrade and smiled. In a faded red and black Bermuda College T-shirt and ragged jeans, his bare feet bronze against the oak flooring, he looked more like the beach bum she remembered than the suited executive she'd found so intimidating in London.

'So what do you think? Better than the hut, right?'

She swung round to take in the view and give herself a moment to regain the power of speech. Expensive, luxury furnishings—including a couple of deep-seated leather sofas, a huge flatscreen TV, a bar framed in glass bricks and a walled fireplace—adorned the tidy, minimalist living area. She stepped through the open doors onto the deck, hoping that the sea breeze would cool the heat rising up her neck. And spotted the edge of an infinity pool, sparkling on the terrace below the house. Steps carved into the stone led down through the grove of palms and banana trees, probably to the beach at Half-Moon Cove.

The cosy, ramshackle beach hut where they'd conceived their child had to be down there somewhere—but felt light years away from the elegance of his real home.

'It's incredibly beautiful. You must have worked very hard to earn all this in under a decade.'

He joined her on the deck, resting his elbows on the rail beside her hip and making her heartbeat spike.

'So you've been checking up on me?'

She studied the sun-bleached hair on his muscular forearms—lost for words again.

She'd expected to be a little intimidated by his wealth—especially after the first class travel over. She hadn't expected to feel completely overwhelmed. Not just by the staggering beauty of his home, but by him too. And the staggering effect he still had on her.

'The Internet is a glorious thing,' she murmured.

Unfortunately all the articles and news clippings about the meteoric rise of his business had contained virtually no information about his personal life. Or his past—bar a few photos of him escorting model-perfect women to island events. And once she'd discovered those, her enthusiasm for playing Nancy Drew had waned considerably.

'The journalist from *Investment* magazine said you were the Rags-to-Riches King of the Islands,' she said. 'She seemed very impressed with your business model.' And not just his business model, Ella had decided, from all the detailed prose about his muscular physique and sparklingly intelligent gaze.

The grin as he glanced her way was quick and boyish. 'Yeah, I remember her. As I recall she hit on me.'

'I'm not sure I needed to know that,' she blurted, before getting control of the sting of jealousy.

He straightened away from the rail. 'Just so you know, I didn't hit on her back.' He skimmed a knuckle down her cheek. 'I like to be the one doing the chasing.' He tucked his finger under her chin. 'Except when it comes to pretty little English cougars who go trawling in beach bars.'

Her pulse sped up to thud against her neck, and the spot between her thighs melted. 'I didn't come back to Bermuda to hit on you again,' she said, trying hard to sound as if she meant it. Sleeping with him would only distract her from the real reason she was here.

He clasped the rail on either side of her hips, boxing her in.

'Then how about I hit on you?'

She gasped as he pressed warm, firm lips to her neck. Lust shot through her like a jolt of electricity—connecting the soft tissue under her chin to the bundle of nerves that lay dormant in her sex.

Except, it wasn't dormant any more.

The sensations spread like molten lava, incinerating everything they touched as he explored her mouth in bold, determined strokes.

She sucked on his tongue, savouring the tangy flavour of him, the groan of desperation. Her fingers flexed against the lean muscles of his abdomen as roughened palms stroked under her blouse. His fingers wrapped around her waist to yank her closer. She shuddered, her sensitive, pregnancy-engorged breasts pressed against the hard wall of his chest.

Sure fingers cupped her breast, then tugged at one hard peak and hot need arrowed down to her sex, the desire erupting like a volcano.

'Wait, Coop.' She wrenched herself free. 'Please, stop

a moment. I need…' She sucked in a breath, her lungs on fire, alongside the rest of her. 'I didn't come for this.'

Did she?

But as his heavy-lidded gaze met hers the heady rush that had been lapping at her senses ever since the car had pulled up to the house surged.

'So what?' He clasped her hand, and headed for the staircase.

He took the stairs two at a time. She could have resisted, could have told him no, but instead she found her feet racing to keep up with him.

He led her into a wide room on the first floor, with a huge four-poster bed draped with gauzy white curtains, and double doors that opened out onto a veranda.

He tugged her into his arms. 'I want you,' he murmured, his voice so low she almost couldn't hear it above the distant sound of the ocean, and the pounding in her eardrums. 'You want me.' His gaze dropped to her midriff. 'We've made a kid together. Why shouldn't we do this?'

She couldn't find a coherent response as the desperate desire to be touched, to be taken in that wild way only he seemed capable of, consumed her.

He jerked off his T-shirt, kicked off his jeans, and then wrestled off her clothes before lifting her, naked and yearning, onto the bed.

Her hands splayed across his wide chest, sank into the blond curls of hair across his nipples. She had to slow him down. Get her mind to engage.

Ruby had warned her not to get distracted, not to fall straight into bed with him. And here she was, less than an hour off the plane and already naked and willing.

'Shouldn't we think about this?' She struggled to hold him back, but the question broke on a soft sob as he cupped her mound. Blunt fingers probed the slick flesh, gliding over the perfect spot.

She bucked, cried out, pleasure radiating across her skin.

The light in his eyes became feral in its intensity. 'You're soaking wet, Ella. What's there to think about?'

Her breath rasped out as he stroked her into a frenzy, caressing the burning nub. Then rolled her over onto her stomach. Raising her hips, he positioned her on all fours, the thick erection nudging her entrance.

'I'll be gentle.' He lifted her hair off her neck, cradled her body with his to nip her shoulder. 'I promise.' Her heavy breasts swayed and he captured them, holding her steady. 'Now tell me you don't want this as much as I do?'

'You know I do.' She moaned, stretched unbearably, as he plunged. Her pulse thundered like an express train in her ears.

Need and desperation pummelled her. She couldn't breathe, couldn't think, the coil yanking tight inside her as he began to move. Pulling out, thrusting back, going impossibly deep, the rhythm torturously slow but steady, relentless, stealing her breath. Her hands fisted in the bedclothes, her body battered by the building waves of pleasure. Sure fingers squeezed her nipples, then he reached down, to open her folds and touch the too-sensitive nub of her clitoris.

Pain and pleasure combined as he shot her to peak. The titanic wave crashed over her as his rhythm built and accelerated. She heard him shout, getting even bigger inside her, before the hot seed pumped into her. He let her go at last and she collapsed onto the bed, her body shaky, her mind dazed, her heart pounding against her ribs with the force and fury of a wrecking ball.

She rolled away from him, feeling stupidly fragile. 'You didn't use any protection,' she murmured.

'Not much point now. That horse has already bolted.' He whispered the words against her ear as his forearm wrapped around her waist and his body cradled her. 'You okay? I didn't hurt you, did I? I was trying to be gentle but I got kind of carried away towards the end.'

She shook her head, struggling to talk round what felt like a wad of cotton wool in her throat. 'No. It felt good.' And scarily intense.

One large hand cupped her breast, his thumb grazing the sensitive nipple. She flinched, the stiff peak too tender for attention.

'I'm sorry.' His thumbs drew back, to trace slow circles around the areola, avoiding the tip. 'The plan wasn't to jump you straight off. But I've missed you.'

'The plan...' She lurched onto her back, dislodging his hand. 'You planned this?'

'Yeah. I guess so.' He propped himself up on an elbow to look down at her, his gaze roaming over her face. 'Why? Is that a problem?'

'I don't know.' She tried to gather her thoughts and make sense of them, while the rush of afterglow still pumped through her system. 'I just thought...'

'What? That this wouldn't happen?' He brushed his fingers across her forehead, tucked the tendrils of hair that had escaped her updo behind her ear. 'Honey, I figure whenever we're on the same continent it's sort of inevitable. So why fight it?'

It wasn't the answer she had been looking for, the one she thought she should have wanted. But as soon as he said it she knew it was the truth.

'Yes, but...' She stared at him. 'That really isn't the reason I came here.'

'So why did you come?'

With her sex still aching from the intensity of their lovemaking, her breasts tender from the pinch of his fingers, and emotion coursing through her system, the answer didn't come as easily as it had when she had been lying in that fold-down bed across the Atlantic.

'To get to know you,' she murmured. 'To find out if you want to be a dad. How involved you want to be. I don't want sex to complicate that.'

'To complicate it?' He chuckled. 'The way I see it, sex is pretty much the only simple thing there is about all this. And we're good at it.' He shrugged, his gaze flicking to her midriff. 'We're going to have to work on the other stuff, because I don't have any easy answers for you there.'

For a moment he looked lost, and the lump of emotion became impossible to swallow down. Was she pushing him too hard, expecting too much, by being here?

'You don't know how you feel about the baby?' she asked, feeling foolish and a little ashamed of her naivety. Why had she been so quick to assume his decision to invite her here meant he must already have feelings for the baby? He'd been thrown into this situation against his will. Of course he'd be confused, maybe even a little resentful.

'Not really.' He flopped back on the bed, stared at the canopy above their heads. 'All I know is I don't want to mess up, like my old man did.'

She turned to him, ready to probe a little. 'How did your father mess up?'

His gaze locked with hers and for a moment she thought she saw something, but then it flicked away again. 'By not being there, I guess. I never met him. It was just my mom and me.'

'I'm sorry.' Her heart sank at the defensive 'don't go there' tone. And the news that he had been abandoned as a child by his own father. No wonder he'd reacted so violently to the news of her pregnancy. Had the horror she'd thought she'd seen been nothing more than blind panic?

She touched his forearm. 'You're not like that. If that's what you're worried about? Because you're already trying to do the right thing.'

He looked at where her fingers touched his arm, then

up at her face, his expression blank now and unreadable. 'You always this much of an optimist?'

His tone was flat, but she refused to let it bother her.

'I try to be,' she said, smiling. 'I don't consider that a bad thing.'

She wanted this child; he was still coming to terms with the fact of it. She had to remember that. Give him time. And space. And not give up hope. His cynicism made complete sense, now she'd had that brief glimpse into his childhood.

'So, what was your mother like?' she asked.

He shook his head, smiling back at her. 'Forget it, Little Miss Sunshine. How about you tell me something about your folks, first? I don't see why I have to do all the talking.'

He'd hardly told her anything, she thought, but she didn't call him on it. Surely telling him more about herself could only increase the intimacy between them, and make it easier for him to open up too?

'Okay, well…' She paused, his question triggering memories of a time in her life that she barely remembered now, but had been so painful once. 'Funnily enough, I think it was watching my parents and seeing what they went through that made me an optimist.'

'How come?'

'Because they had an incredibly acrimonious divorce when I was eight.'

His eyebrows shot up. 'And that made you an optimist?'

'Well, yes. Because it taught me how important second chances are,' she continued, choosing to ignore the sceptical expression. 'They'd tried to stay together for me and my brother and it had been a disaster. Children always see more than you think.' She sighed, remembering the whisper arguments, the bitter silences, the terror and confusion when she and her brother had been told Daddy would be moving out. 'I missed my dad terribly and it was awful to see my mum so sad and angry all the time. But then, eventually, they both found the people they were meant to be with. And I ended up with a stepmum who makes to-die-for chocolate cake and a stepdad who drove me and Ruby to cookery fairs without complaint. It totally transformed them both, made them much better people and much better parents. Because they were finally happy.'

He rolled onto his side, and suddenly she became aware of his nakedness, and hers, and the low-level hum of arousal that always seemed to be there. He placed a warm palm on her hip, slid it up to cup her breast. 'That's sweet,' he said, the comment only mildly condescending. Then he ducked his head, to lick a pouting nipple. 'But not as sweet as you are. You know, your breasts look incredible. Have they got bigger?'

Right, it seemed their deep and meaningful conversation appeared to be over. She knew a distraction technique when she heard one—and felt it hardening against her hip.

'Yes, they have...'

He leant down and sucked at the tip of her breast, gently, provocatively.

'The obstetrician says it's to do with the pregnancy hormones,' she continued, trying to focus despite the glorious feel of her nipple swelling against his tongue. 'They're much more sensitive too.'

He grinned up at her. 'Awesome.'

Wrapping his lips around the stiffened peak, he drew it against the roof of his mouth. Her fingers plunged into his hair as she held his head and gasped, the pleasure almost too intense to bear now. 'Oh, God...'

His growing erection nudged her belly, and she reached to stroke the shaft instinctively. But as she brushed her thumb across the bead of liquid at the head, rejoicing at his growl of need, her stomach rumbled loudly.

'Enough.' He gave a strained laugh, carefully dislodging her hand. Then kissed her fingers, his smile mocking. 'I guess I'm going to have to offer you food. I don't want you passing out your first day.'

At the mention of food, her stomach growled again. Colour tainted her cheeks as he laughed. 'How about you go grab a shower, and I'll put out the food my housekeeper prepared for us? We can eat out on the deck.'

'I'd like that,' she said, suddenly grateful for the respite, and the chance to examine all the emotions careering through her system.

Although she'd discovered in the last twenty minutes that he had a few 'issues' about his role as a father to overcome, it felt good to have got her first proper glimpse of the man behind the confident façade he wore so well. And exciting to know that they'd already started to establish a new intimacy between them.

Despite all Ruby's dire warnings not to confuse her joy about the pregnancy with anything else, she wasn't the least bit worried about jumping back into bed with Coop.

The one good thing about her terrible experience with Randall was, she'd never be delusional enough to mistake hot sex for love again.

Just because Coop looked great, smelled amazing, knew how to hit all her happy buttons—endorphin-wise—had sperm supersonic enough to impregnate her virtually barren body, and made everything inside her gather and tighten when he looked at her a certain way, she knew she could remain totally objective about their relationship. Such as it was.

Her main priority was the baby. And that would never change.

She lay back in the bed, and took a moment to appreciate the delicious view of Coop's naked backside as he tugged his jeans back on. And stifled the sigh as the pale strip of defined muscle disappeared behind battered denim.

Her stomach fluttered as if it were filled with hyperactive butterflies when he leaned down to press a kiss to her lips. 'Supper will be served in twenty minutes, Little Miss Sunshine. Don't be late.'

'Aye aye, Captain.'

He strolled out, and her gaze dipped back down to that beautifully tight butt—while the swooping sensation in her stomach bottomed out.

Okay, maybe sleeping with Coop would be a tiny bit distracting, but surely they were going to need some light relief from all the heavy stuff they had to deal with? And the truth was, the intimacy of sex seemed to be a great way to get him to lower his guard.

She squinted as the setting sun dipped lower and the light peaked past the four-poster's gauzy curtains onto the bed. In fact, now she thought about it, maybe she should consider it her duty to seduce him as often as possible.

Damn, you nearly blew it.

Coop put the last of the platters Inez had prepared on the outdoor table. The generous plate of lobster salad, Inez's salted crab cakes and colourful sides of fruit salsa, fried plantain and cornbread had saliva gathering under his tongue.

Good, hopefully Inez's mouth-watering spread would keep his mouth and hands busy when Ella came down for her supper. He uncorked a chilled bottle of Pouilly Fuissé and splashed a couple of slugs into a glass before planting the bottle in the ice bucket next to the table.

Time to cool the hell down.

What the hell had got into him? He'd seen her less than a week ago. Had made love to her less than ten days ago. And yet, he'd jumped her as soon as she'd arrived.

One gasp of breath, one look from those trusting eyes and he'd been all over her like a rash. His first night with her had already caused more problems than he knew how to solve. And now he was losing all his cool points too? What the hell?

He gulped the pricey wine without tasting a single drop—the thought of the baby going some way to dousing the heat in his pants.

She loved this kid already; he could see it in the dreamy look every time she mentioned it. And then there were all those questions about how he felt about the baby. Making him pretty sure she wasn't going to be impressed with his initial thought that maybe his role in the child's life could be limited to setting up a hefty college fund and giving her a monthly allowance to cover her expenses.

On the balcony above, the white cotton curtains billowed out of the open balcony doors caught by the early evening breeze off the ocean. The sound of running water drifted down from the guest room's shower.

The image of Ella, naked and flushed, her rosy nipples begging to be sucked, swirled into his brain.

He drained the glass. Snagged one of the patties off the plate, wrapped it in some arugula and stuffed it in his mouth.

Enjoy it, Delaney, because crab cakes are the only cakes you're going to be sucking on for the rest of the night.

He needed to keep his wits about him. And not fall into the trap of getting hot and heavy about anything other than the sex. Until he had some answers to Ella's questions.

With that in mind…

Picking his smartphone off the table, he keyed in his housekeeper's home number. When Inez picked up he told her to take a holiday for a couple of weeks, all expenses paid. He could hear the suspicion in the older woman's voice—Inez had six grown kids and eight grandbabies and was nobody's fool—but after checking he'd remember to water the plants and suggesting a local girl to come in and do the laundry and cleaning while she was away, she finally took the bait.

Then he rang Sonny, listened to a lengthy update on the wedding arrangements, and then told his friend that he wouldn't be around for a while and if he needed anyone to help out with tours to contact his business manager. Then he carefully layered in a request to tell Josie he'd be mostly off island till the wedding.

He knew Josie was likely to be his biggest problem. Like any annoying little sister, that girl was more curious than the proverbial cat, had got into the bad habit of thinking she could drop in on him any time unannounced—and had an even bigger mouth than Inez.

He tucked the phone into the back pocket of his jeans. And dispelled the small tug of guilt. Ella would get to meet all his friends at Josie's wedding in three weeks' time if she was still here, but until then it would be better if they both kept a low profile.

Their little heart-to-heart and that poignant insight into her childhood had been unsettling and he didn't want any more weird moments like that again if he could avoid them.

When she'd told him about her parents' break-up, the urge to take away the unhappiness in her eyes had been dumb enough. But much worse had been the freaky feeling of connection. Because he remembered exactly what it was like to be scared, to be confused, to feel as if your world were being ripped apart and there wasn't a damn thing you could do about it. When he was a child, his mother's black moods, those dark days when she couldn't function, or when she cried—usually after his father had been by to screw her for old times' sake—had scared the hell out of him.

He'd almost told Ella about it. Thank God, he'd managed to stop himself just in time. Because the last thing he needed was them sharing confidences about stuff that meant nothing now.

He'd ridden out the storm long ago and he'd survived. And Ella had too.

But, unlike Ella, his takeaway from his childhood had been nowhere near as sunny and sweet as hers. And that made her vulnerable in a way he hadn't really considered until now.

Ella was an optimist, unrealistic expectations came with the territory, and he didn't want her getting any unrealistic ideas about him and what he was able to offer her and the kid.

But that didn't mean he didn't enjoy seeing that bright light in her eyes, or knowing she thought more of him than he knew was there. He certainly didn't plan to extinguish that light unnecessarily. Plus, after way too many bruising fights and angry words in his youth, and all those endless pointless arguments with his mom to get her to see the truth about his old man, he'd also become a big fan of avoidance when it came to talking about your feelings.

Especially if you had nothing to say on the matter.

Getting Ella together with Sonny and Josie and telling them about the baby would just create loads of unnecessary drama. He shivered as goosebumps pebbled down his spine at the thought. Because neither one of them could keep their noses out of his business and they had an opinion about every damn thing. And Inez was one of the biggest gossips on the island, so it made sense to keep her out of the loop too. He didn't want anyone knowing his business before he knew it himself.

He put the glass down at the soft pad of footsteps on the stairs and glanced up, his pulse slowing to a harsh, jerky beat as Ella walked towards him.

The filmy dress she wore blew around her legs. The

bodice only showed a small amount of cleavage, but he could still make out that magnificent rack and the bullet-tipped nipples outlined by the snug fabric.

Well, he guessed that was some compensation—however many problems this pregnancy was going to cause in the long term, he could totally get behind the changes his child was making to her body now.

He put a dampener on the thought when she opened her mouth in a jaw-breaking yawn. He needed to keep his dick under control tonight, at least until she'd slept off the effects of her flight. And suffering through another sleepless night might make him think twice before losing his cool with her again.

'Hi, this looks amazing,' she said, surveying the table. 'I'm so hungry I could eat a horse.'

'You're not the only one.'

She laughed, that musical lilt that had beguiled him from the get-go. 'Why do I have the strange feeling it's not a horse you want to eat?'

Smart girl.

He took her hand, kissed the knuckles. 'As much as I'd like to eat you, tonight, it's probably best if you stay in the guest room.' He pulled out her chair so she could take a seat. 'Alone.' He bit down on the groan as she tucked the pretty dress round that tempting butt.

'You don't have to do that.' The furrow of surprise and disappointment on her brow was almost comical. 'Unless you want to,' she added, as if his wanting her was actually in doubt.

'Honey, you've just got off an eight-hour flight.' He forced himself to be noble and ignore the growing ache in his crotch. 'It's the early hours by my count in the UK and...' He was about to point out that she was pregnant, but stopped himself. No need to bring up that topic unnecessarily. 'And I don't want to wear you out,' he finished.

The heart-pumping smile brightened her whole face. 'That's very considerate of you.' Wasn't it just? 'But I should warn you, I'm not good with jet lag. I'll probably wake up at the crack of dawn.'

He allowed himself a firm kiss, of exactly two seconds' duration. Because any longer would only increase the torment. 'Once you're awake, you'll find me in the bedroom at the end of the veranda.' Most likely wide awake and ready for action. 'I'm sure I can figure out a way to cure your jet lag.' She blushed prettily and his voice lowered. 'Sleep therapy happens to be a speciality of mine.'

'I'll bet.' The eagerness on her face crucified him. 'I'm sure that will come in handy, come cougar time.'

He chuckled, the sound rough, as he pulled up a chair and began piling the food onto their plates. He listed the different dishes Inez had prepared, reeled off some suggested activities she might like to try in the next couple of days, and neatly sidestepped a couple of questions about the snorkel tour. And Sonny.

To stay focused on eating the food and not her, he kept in mind that, while tonight would be torture, downtime now would be rewarded by lots of uptime from tomorrow morning onwards.

He quizzed her about her business and as many other generic topics as he could think of before her eyelids began to droop. He showed her back up to the guest bed after supper, and kissed her on the cheek—and had to be grateful that she was too exhausted to do more than smile sleepily back. Especially when her scent invaded his nostrils, and it took every last ounce of his will power to step back and close the door after her. Just before the door clicked shut, he heard the soft sound of her flopping onto the bed they'd shared less than an hour ago—and his knuckles whitened on the door handle.

It took a couple of seconds but he finally let go.

Tucking his clenched fists into his pockets, he headed down the hall to the library at the other end of the house, feeling more noble than Sir Galahad.

Booting up the computer on his desktop, he ran a search on the effects of pregnancy on a woman's body in the first and second trimester. Might be good to do some research—Ella said sex in pregnancy was safe, but, considering how much sex they were likely to want, he didn't want to be making any demands on her she couldn't handle.

But he couldn't concentrate on the information, his impatience for the night to be over growing as the endless minutes ticked by. The thought that every one of those minutes shortened the time they had left together only irritated him more.

What was up with that?

They had as much time as they needed. She'd agreed to buy an open ticket. And very few women had kept his interest for more than a couple of dates. So it stood to reason that, no matter how cute and fascinating and hot he found her, or how much baggage they had to sort out with the baby, having her in his home would get old soon enough.

So why the heck was he was already worrying about her departure?

CHAPTER TEN

'WOW, THAT WAS *A-MAZING*!' Ella shoved up her mask and hit the release button on her tanks. She laughed, her mind still reeling from all the images she'd seen and absorbed in the last thirty minutes. She'd thought snorkelling on the reef had been a lifetime experience, but her first scuba-dive had topped it.

Darting fish, waving coral, the dappled sunlight shining through the waves and the pure white sand sparkling under her flippers.

'Here. Let me.' Coop grabbed the air tanks and set them on the boat's deck before shrugging off his own equipment.

'I almost had a cow when I saw that shark.' She shuddered, the laugh breathless at the memory of the majestic creature gliding by beneath them. 'What kind was it? It looked enormous.'

She unzipped the snug wetsuit, struggled out of the top half.

'Tiger shark, about seven feet.' Cooper sent her a mocking smile as he climbed out of his own suit. Water glistened on his tanned chest, diverting her gaze. 'Not much more than a baby. Nothing to freak out about.'

'You're joking—that was no baby,' she replied, indignant. 'And I didn't freak out.' *Much.*

He chuckled and grabbed her wrist, to pull her into his embrace. 'I guess you handled yourself pretty well.'

His palm touched her cheek and she felt the giddy rush of pleasure from the intense study. 'For a rookie,' he whispered, before his lips covered hers and she forgot to be mad.

They were both breathless when they came up for air. Her heart beat in an even more irregular rhythm than when she'd spotted the tiger shark.

'So, you want to do that again some time?' His hands settled on her waist, his thumbs brushing her hips above the half-off wetsuit. 'Sharks notwithstanding.'

'Yes, please. And I loved the shark.' He chuckled at her enthusiasm. 'It was so beautiful and exciting.'

But not as beautiful and exciting as you, she almost added, but stopped herself just in time. She'd been on the island ten days now, and it was getting harder and harder not to let her feelings run away with themselves. With his damp hair falling across his brow, those handsome features gilded by sunlight, and the lean muscles of his six-pack rigid against her palms it was even harder to remember why she shouldn't let them.

She'd had an incredible time so far. When she'd been here in April, she'd stayed almost exclusively at the resort. And had no idea that she'd missed so much of what the island had to offer. The colonial elegance of the pastel-shaded houses and cobblestoned streets in St George, the exhilaration of a motorbike ride to a secluded cove, the luxury of an impromptu picnic lunch at a beach café.

But best of all had been Coop's attention and his willingness to spend so much time with her. Every day he'd laid on a new adventure to experience. And apart from a few hours spent in his study each day to deal with his business, he'd hardly left her side.

She hadn't expected him to be this enthusiastic about showing her around—or how much she would enjoy his company. She felt young and carefree and bold, excited at the prospect of trying out new things that she might have been too cautious to try out before.

Yesterday morning he'd announced she was learning to scuba-dive. Then he'd devoted most of the day to teaching her. Fitting her out while demonstrating all the equipment, giving her endless lessons in how to breathe through the regulator in the pool, running through all the safety routines, and the intricacies of buddy breathing.

They'd managed a short training dive yesterday from the beach, but today he'd taken her out on the motor cruiser.

And the thirty-minute dive had been spectacular. Every second of it.

But even her first scuba-dive in Bermuda couldn't top the wonder of spending her nights and the long lazy mornings in bed with Coop. The man had skills in the bedroom that were quite simply phenomenal—making love to her with care and dedication one minute and hungry intensity the next.

Of course, during all the fun and frolics, she'd been careful to keep reminding herself that this trip wasn't about her and Coop but about the baby—which hadn't been all that hard to do, for the simple reason that she hadn't made a lot of progress in that area at all.

He talked about their baby and the pregnancy, but only in very generic, impersonal ways. In fact, he was so guarded on the subject whenever it came up now, that she had begun to wonder if all the new activities, all the wonderful experiences hadn't been arranged to distract her from any mention of why she was really here.

She hated herself for being suspicious of his motives, for doubting his sincerity in any way, but most of all she didn't understand why he would even want to do that. What possible reason could he have to avoid the subject? When he'd invited her to his home specifically to talk about it? It didn't make any sense.

'You want to go back out tomorrow?' he asked, brushing her hair back from her face.

The flutter of contentment pushed aside the foolish moment of doubt.

She was being ridiculous. How could he be avoiding talking to her, when they were together so much of the time? 'Could we go out again today?'

He tapped her nose. 'No way. Half an hour's enough. You're a beginner and...' his gaze flicked to her abdomen and he took his hand from her waist '...you know.'

It was an oblique reference to the baby, but a reference nonetheless, so she decided to go with it. If she had concerns, maybe it was about time she voiced them. She knew she had a tendency to avoid confrontations. Probably a layover from her early childhood, when her parents had spent so much of the time arguing—and the hideous breakdown of her relationship with Randall.

But if the thought of the baby made Coop uncomfortable, the only way to get over that was to stop letting him avoid the subject. And when she'd Skyped Ruby the day before, her friend had told her in no uncertain terms to stop worrying and confront Coop about the issue.

'I called the obstetrician this morning,' she said as casually as she could manage. 'The one you lined up for me. She said scuba-diving would be absolutely fine.'

'Yeah, you told me. But it's still not a good idea to push it.'

'I didn't know you'd heard me,' she said, trying not to mind the abrupt dismissal as he set about hanging the air tanks on their frame. 'I arranged to go in for a check-up on Monday, by the way,' she added, but he didn't look up, engrossed in checking the gauges. 'If you want to come with me?'

That had got his attention, she thought, as his head shot

up. 'Why?' There was no mistaking the flicker of panic. 'Do I need to? Is there something wrong?'

'No, of course not, but...' While his concern warmed her, the panic was another matter. 'I thought you might like to come—she might do a scan and you could see the baby.'

'Right.' He turned away, went back to concentrating on the equipment. 'Why don't you shimmy out of that wet-suit?' He threw the request over his shoulder. 'Then we can head back before you start to burn. It's hot as hell out here.'

She inched the wetsuit down her legs, sat down on the boat's bench seat to struggle out of the clinging black neo-prene. 'So you'll come to the scan? On Monday?'

She handed him the suit and he draped it over the bench seat next to his.

'Yeah, maybe, I don't know. I'll have to see how I'm fixed.' He met her eyes at last, the 'don't get too excited' tone in his voice loud and clear. 'When's your appoint-ment?'

The lack of enthusiasm was almost palpable and she had the sudden premonition that he was only asking for the in-formation so he had time to come up with a viable excuse.

'Two-thirty.'

'Damn, that's a shame. I promised Sonny I'd come over that afternoon. I'll have to miss it.'

Her heart stuttered. So now she knew for sure. She had not imagined his reluctance. She drew in a deep breath, determined not to back down again in the face of his stub-bornness.

'I see.' She tugged her beach tunic on over her bikini, the ocean breeze making her shiver despite the heat. 'I could rearrange the appointment for later. Why don't I come with you to see Sonny? I'd love to meet him.'

The sides of his mouth pinched—making the strain to maintain the easy smile on his lips more visible. 'No need for that. I'm helping him strip an old motor. It's not going to be any fun.'

She felt the dismissal like a slap that time. She'd asked before about his friends on the island. And he'd closed her down on that subject too. She'd been here for over a week and she hadn't met anyone he knew. When she'd suggested going back to The Rum Runner the previous evening, he'd explained that he didn't want Henry hitting on her again, then picked her up and dumped her in the pool. Once he'd dived in after her and then 'helped' her out of her wet clothes, the request had quickly been forgotten.

She watched as he began to pack the equipment into the box at the end of the boat. The panicked beat of her heart richocheted against her chest wall.

Stop freaking out and ask him. Avoidance isn't the answer. You can't handle this if you don't know what's going on.

'Don't you want me to meet your friends?'

He swung round on his haunches, his eyebrow arching up his forehead. 'Huh?'

'It just seems a bit strange—' she forced the comment out, past lips that had dried to parchment '—that wherever we go we never seem to bump into anyone you know.'

She saw the flash of guilt in his eyes before he was able to mask it.

'They don't even know I'm here, do they?' she asked, but from the flags of colour on his tanned cheeks she already knew the answer. The fact that he hadn't told anyone about the baby either went without saying. She clamped down on the feeling of unease though. She mustn't overreact. Just because he hadn't told them yet, didn't mean he would never tell them.

He swore softly and stood up. 'Not yet.'

'I see.' She swallowed. 'Do you plan to tell people? Eventually?'

'Yeah, sure. I just wanted to keep you to myself for a while.' He held her arm, his voice lowering to a seductive purr as he caressed the sensitive skin on the inside of her elbow with his thumb. 'You remember Josie, Sonny's daughter, the kid that woke you up when you were in the hut?'

She nodded.

'She's having a big wedding on the beach next Saturday. We'll have to go to that, I'm one of the witnesses. Everyone will be there.'

He went back to sorting out the equipment.

'Oh, okay. That's good,' she said, although the way he'd said they would 'have to go' made it sound as if he wasn't too happy at the prospect. 'But it might be nice to see them before that?' she pushed. Obviously she had overreacted, but something about the whole thing still bothered her. Was he planning to keep their relationship a secret until then? 'Because, you know, it might be a bit weird me turning up at this wedding pregnant with your child, if no one knows me.'

'Do you think they'll be able to tell?' He dropped the wetsuit he'd been packing as his eyes shot down to her tummy. 'You're not showing too much yet.'

What?

The feeling of unease was replaced by the shock of vulnerability.

'Well, no, maybe not, but…' The words got caught behind the silly lump of emotion. Which had to be the pregnancy hormones, making her feel ridiculously oversensitive. But she couldn't stop the thoughts coming, now that the dam had broken. 'Why don't you want them to know?'

'Hey, what's the matter?' He stood up, the concern in his eyes almost making her back down again. 'It's not that big a deal. Believe me, it's just easier not to tell them yet.'

She stared at him. Was he actually serious?

Yes, it might make it easier for him, but how would it be easier for her? Wouldn't it make things awkward at this wedding if someone did notice? And asked questions about her condition? She knew they weren't a proper couple, that she shouldn't get too invested in their relationship. That they were just having fun with each other while sorting out what to do about their shared child. But the fact was, she'd been here for ten days, and they hadn't actually sorted out anything yet. Not even how he was going to introduce her to his friends.

Was she his girlfriend? His wedding date? A holiday fling? Or just another of his temporary bonk buddies? Maybe being the mother of his child didn't give her any relationship rights, but surely it ought to afford her a tiny iota of respect?

'The thing is, Coop,' she began, trying not to let the hurt show, 'I can't see how not talking about the baby is making it easier for me. I can't stay here indefinitely, you know, and—'

'Damn it, Ella, you've only been here a week. We can't rush this stuff.'

'*Rush it*? Coop, I've been here ten days!' she said, exasperated now. 'And we haven't talked about the baby at all.'

'Because we've been busy, doing…' he paused '…other stuff,' he said, so emphatically that she suddenly realised she'd been right to be suspicious of the endless round of activities. 'Stuff that you said you enjoyed,' he added, grudgingly, sounding a little hurt.

'I did enjoy them. I loved every single minute of them,' she rushed to reassure him, but then noticed he didn't actually look *that* hurt. 'But that's not the point. We could have talked about it in the mornings before we went out. Or in the evenings when we got back.'

'Uh-huh, well, we've been pretty busy then too.' His

gaze raked down her figure, making her whole body warm. And it occurred to her that the relentless schedule of day-time activities might not have been his only distraction technique. 'And I don't recall you complaining about that either,' he added. 'Especially when I had my mouth on that succulent little clit this morning.'

Hell. That did it.

She glared at him—the succulent nub in question throb-bing alarmingly now in unison with her distended nipples. 'You sod.' He'd been playing her all along. And she'd been too dazed by her own lust to see it. 'You've been seducing me deliberately, haven't you, to stop me from discussing it? I knew it.'

'Hey, calm down. I have not.' His lips quirked. 'I love sucking on your clitoris, remember?' He reached for her arm, but she jerked it out of his grasp. Not finding the joke—or the fact that her clitoris wouldn't stop throb-bing—remotely amusing any more.

'I suppose the next question is why? Why would you do that? Unless…' Her temper faded, and then collapsed, at the stubborn, defensive look on his face.

Oh, no. Not that.

She heaved a heavy sigh when he didn't say anything, scared to say it, terrified that she might be right, but know-ing she had to ask. 'If you're having second thoughts about being involved with this baby, Coop, you need to tell me.' She met his gaze, the flags of colour on his cheeks shin-ing beneath his tan. 'I want you to be part of its life, very much.'

Maybe she still didn't know much about how he really felt about parenthood, but the things she had learned about him in the last week had convinced her of that much. His generosity, his intelligence, the quick wit that always made her laugh, the care he took with her, his need to look out for her and protect her and the capable, patient way he'd taught her how to scuba-dive, not to mention that reck-less, dangerously exciting streak that made her feel bold too, made her sure he would make a wonderful father. 'I'm not here to force a connection on you that you don't feel.'

She couldn't make him want to be a father, however much she might want to. That wouldn't be fair on him, and it certainly wouldn't be fair on her child.

'If you're not ready to discuss this yet, it's probably best if I just leave.'

The calm, rhythmic sound of the ocean lapping against the side of the boat stretched across the silence. She flinched as he raked his fingers through his hair and broke the silence with a bitter curse.

What the hell did he say to that?

She was looking at him with those big round trust-ing eyes. And he knew he hadn't been honest with her, or with himself.

But he didn't want her to leave. Not yet. He wasn't ready. And he did want to figure out what to do about the kid. But the more she'd talked about the baby, the more inadequate it had made him feel, until the problem had become so huge he'd clammed up completely. Plus, it had been so damn easy just to get lost in her and forget about all that. She was so cute and funny and engaging. Every-thing he showed her she loved; everything they did to-gether she threw herself into with a complete lack of fear. She was smart and funny and resourceful and so eager and responsive. Especially in bed.

But she was right: he'd played her, even if he hadn't really intended to. And now he owed her an explanation.

'Come here, Ella.' He tried to take her into his arms, the guilt tightening his throat when she grasped his fore-arms to hold him off.

'Please, just give me a straight answer, Coop. Don't try to sugar-coat it, okay. I can take it.'

He wasn't so sure of that. 'I swear, no more messing you about.'

He sat on the boat's bench seat, and gently pulled her into his lap, pathetically grateful when she didn't resist him again.

'There's no need to make up excuses.' She cupped his cheek and the guilt peaked. 'I understand if you feel over-whelmed.'

He covered her hand and dragged it away from her face. 'Stop being so damn reasonable, Ella.'

She stiffened in his arms. 'This isn't about being rea-sonable. It's about being fair. I don't want to force you to shoulder a responsibility you don't want.'

'Damn it, Ella, who the hell ever told you life was fair?'

It scared him how easily she could be crushed, espe-cially by a guy like him—who always looked out for him-self first.

She tried to rise, but he held her tight, pressed his fore-head into her shoulder. 'I'm sorry, don't go…' He sucked in a deep breath, prepared to admit at least some of the truth, even though the feel of her butt nestled against his groin was having a predictable effect.

What he wouldn't give right now to strip off the light cotton dress and feast on her lush body—and get the hell out of this conversation. But he couldn't carry on lying to her.

He rested his head back against the seat. Stared at the blue sky, the swooping seagulls, the clean bright sunlight. And felt the darkness he'd spent so long running away from descend over him like a fog.

He forced his head off the seat to look her in the face. 'Hasn't it ever occurred to you that I might not be cut out to be a dad? That you and the kid might be much better off without me?'

'No, it hasn't,' she said and the total confidence in her voice sneaked past all the defences he'd put in place over the years. 'I realise you're not as ecstatic about this pregnancy as I am. But that doesn't mean you won't be a good father when the time comes. If you're willing to try?'

'I want to try, but I just don't know if...'

'There aren't any guarantees, Coop, not when it comes to being a parent. You just have to do what comes naturally and hope for the best.'

'I guess, but you'll be a lot better at that than I am,' he said, able to appreciate the irony.

'Maybe you should ask yourself why you're so insecure about this. Would that help?'

'I doubt it.' He definitely didn't want to go there.

'Is it because of your own father? And the fact that you never knew him?' she said, going there without any help from him. 'Is that it?'

He shook his head. Damn, he'd have to tell her the truth about that too, now. 'I did know him. I guess I lied about that.'

'Oh.' She looked surprised, but not wary. Or not wary yet. 'Why did you lie?' she asked, as if it were the most natural thing in the world.

'Because I didn't exactly *know* him,' he clarified, trying to explain to her something he'd never understood. 'I knew of him. And he knew about me.'

'I don't...' she said, obviously struggling to figure it out.

'I grew up in a small place in Indiana called Garysville,' he said, reciting a story he'd denied for so long, he felt as if he were talking about some other kid's life. 'Towns like that, everyone knows everyone else's business. My old man was the police chief. A big deal with a reputation to protect, who liked to play away from home. Everyone knew I was his kid, because I looked a lot like him. And my mom didn't exactly keep it a secret.'

'But surely you must have talked to him? If it was such a small town.'

And you were his son.

He could hear her thinking it. And remembered all the times he'd tortured himself with the same question as a boy.

'Why would I?' The old bitterness surprised him a little. 'He was just some guy who came over to screw my mother from time to time. She told him I was his. He didn't want to know.'

'He never spoke to you?' She looked horrified. 'But that's hideous—how could he not want to know you?'

Like father, like son, he thought grimly. Wasn't that what he had thought about doing to his own kid? When he'd figured money would be enough to free him of any responsibility for his child.

'Actually, that's not true, I did speak to him once. Six words...' He forced the humiliating memory to the surface, to punish himself. 'You want to know what they were?'

Ella's heart clutched as Coop's face took on a cold, distant expression, the tight smile nothing like the warm, witty man she knew. She nodded, although she wasn't sure she did want to know. He seemed so unhappy.

'Do you want fries with that?' The brittle half-laugh held no amusement. 'Pretty tragic, isn't it?'

Her heart ached at the flatness of his tone. 'Oh, Coop,' she said, the sharp pain in her chest like a punch. No wonder he was so reluctant to talk about the baby. It wasn't fear of the responsibility; it was simply a lack of confidence.

'I worked nights at a drive-thru in town when I was in high school,' he continued, still talking in that flat, even tone that she was sure now was used to mask his emotions.

'My mom was finding it hard to stay in a job, she had…' he paused. '…these moods.' He shrugged. 'Anyhow we needed the money. He drove in one night with his family, about a month after I'd got the job. He ordered two chilli dogs, two chocolate malts and a side order of onion rings for his kids. Delia and Jack Jnr.'

She wondered if he realised how significant it was that he'd remembered the order exactly. 'You knew them?'

'Sure, we went to the same high school. Not that we moved in the same circles. Delia was the valedictorian, Jack Junior the star quarterback. And I hated their guts, because I was so damn jealous of the money they had, the choices.' He huffed out a bitter laugh. 'And the Beemer convertible Jack Jnr got for his sixteenth birthday.'

And the fact that they had a father, your father, and you didn't, she thought, her heart aching for him.

'He looked me right in the eye and said no, they didn't need fries, then he paid and drove on. He never came to my window again.'

She heard the yearning in his voice and the punch of pain twisted.

No wonder he'd worked so hard to get away from there, to make something out of his life. Rejection always hurt. It had nearly destroyed her when Randall had rejected her, but at least she'd been an adult. Or adult enough. She couldn't imagine suffering that kind of knock-back as a child. Every single day. To have it thrown in your face that you weren't good enough, and never knowing why.

The casual cruelty of the man who had fathered him, but had never had the guts to acknowledge him, disgusted her. But his bravery in rising above it, in overcoming it— surely that was what mattered. Why couldn't he see that?

'But you've got to understand, Ella. I'm not sure I'm a good bet as a father. Because I'm a selfish bastard, just like he was.'

She wanted to tell him that he was wrong. That he wasn't selfish, he was only self-sufficient, because he'd had to be. And that she admired him so much for having the courage to rise above the rejection. But she knew it wasn't only admiration that was making her heart pound frantically in her chest.

She touched his cheek, felt the rasp of the five o'clock shadow already beginning to grow at two in the afternoon. 'Do you really think you're the only one of us who's scared, Coop? The only one who thinks they won't measure up?'

He stared at her. 'Get real, Ella. You've loved this kid from the get-go. You've made it your number one priority from the start.' His gaze roamed over her face. 'How would you feel if I told you I'm pretty sure I only invited you here because I wanted you. Not the kid?' The desire in his heavy-lidded eyes made the heat pulse low in her abdomen. 'If that doesn't tell you what kind of father I'd be, I don't know what the hell does.'

She smiled, utterly touched by the admission. 'Actually I'm flattered. And rather turned on.'

'Seriously, Ella. For once, I'm not kidding around about—'

'I know you're not.' She cut him off, then gripped his cheeks, pressed her forehead against his, and prepared to tell him something she had never wanted him to know. 'How about if I told you that when I was eighteen I got pregnant and I had a termination? Would you still think I don't have some pretty persuasive reasons to doubt my own ability as a parent?'

She forced her gaze to his, willing him not to judge her as harshly as she had always judged herself.

His eyes widened, but he looked more stunned than disgusted. 'That's your big revelation? Big deal. You were eighteen. Why would you want a kid at that age?'

She shook her head. 'But you don't understand. I did

want it.' She rested her palm on her belly, emboldened by the new life growing there to talk for the first time about the one she'd lost. 'I wanted it very much. Which is why this child means so much to me now.'

'Okay, I get that.' He threaded his fingers through hers, the acceptance in his eyes unconditional. 'But you can't punish yourself now for a choice you made at eighteen. Having a baby at that age would have screwed up your life.'

She wanted to take his comfort, his faith in her, but she couldn't, not till he knew the whole truth. 'But that's not why I did it. I had the abortion because Randall ordered me to. He insisted. He said either I lose the baby, or I would lose him. And I chose him. Over my own child.'

A tear slipped over her lid, and he brushed his thumb across her cheek.

'Ella, don't cry.' She heard the tenderness and knew she didn't deserve it. 'This Randall was the father?'

She nodded, tucked her head onto his shoulder. 'Pretty pathetic, isn't it?'

'Not pathetic,' he said, nudging her chin up with his forefinger. 'You were young and scared. And given an impossible choice by that bastard. That's his bad, not yours.'

Ruby had always said the same thing to her, when she'd tortured herself with what ifs after the procedure. But now, for the first time, she felt herself begin to accept it.

Coop rubbed the tight muscles at the base of her neck. 'I'm guessing Randall didn't stick around once he'd got you to do what he wanted.'

'How did you know that?'

'Because the guy sounds like a selfish, manipulative jerk.' He sighed, then brushed her hair off her forehead, and his lips tilted in a wry smile. 'It takes one to know one.'

'You're nothing like him.'

'I don't know—I freaked pretty bad when you told me about Junior. And I've been doing my best to avoid the subject ever since.' He rested his hand on her belly, rubbed it gently back and forth. It was the first time he'd ever touched her there, and the flood of warmth caught her unawares.

'Yes, but you apologised for flipping out the very next day,' she pointed out. 'Even though you were still reeling from the news. And you've never tried to pressure me the way he did. That makes you a much better man than Randall ever was.'

The half-smile became rueful. 'I don't know about that.' She opened her mouth to protest, but he lifted a finger to her lips, silencing her. 'But I'm glad you think so. How about I come to the scan on Monday?'

The smile in her heart at the suggestion was even bigger than the one she could see reflected in his eyes. 'Okay, if you're sure?'

She knew what a big leap this was for him, so she was doubly pleased when he took a deep breath, then nodded. 'I guess so. I can't guarantee I'll know what I'm doing, but I'd like to be there anyway.'

'That's wonderful, Coop.'

His fingers threaded into her hair as he captured her lips in a tender kiss. But what started as gentle, coaxing, quickly heated to carnal as she opened her mouth and flicked her tongue against his.

She felt the satisfying swell of his erection, coming back to life against her bottom as she feasted on him—and let him feast on her.

He drew back first, to flick his thumb across the stiff peak of her nipple. But when she tried to reach for the front of his shorts and the stiff length inside, he grabbed her wrist to hold her off.

'Not a good idea.'

'Why not?' she said, the rush of emotion only intensifying her eagerness.

He kissed her nose. And she felt the tiny sting. 'Because you're getting a little pink around the edges, and I don't want you getting a sunburn. It's liable to cramp our style.'

He lifted her off his lap, to walk to the boat's console.

'Why don't we just go below decks?'

'For what I've got in mind, we're going to need a bigger bed.' He grinned over his shoulder and fired up the boat's engine. 'Now sit down and grab a hold of something. I'm going to see how fast I can get this thing back to base.'

She did as she was told, impossibly pleased that his eagerness matched her own, before he whisked the steering wheel round and hit the accelerator. The rush of wind lifted her hair and made the sunburn on her nose tingle as the launch bounced over the swell, hurtling them back towards the dock below his house at breakneck speed.

Her heart pumped to a deafening crescendo as she held on for dear life and watched him steer with practised ease. And the tightness that she hadn't realised had been making her chest ache for days released. Everything was going to be all right.

She faced into the wind, felt the spray of water hit her cheeks, and gave herself up to the excitement, the exhilaration pumping through her system.

She glanced back as the boat slowed to approach the small dock that stood below the back steps up to his property.

'Tie her up,' he shouted and she grabbed the thin nylon rope, climbed onto the dock and began looping the rope round the post while he switched off the engine.

His gaze locked on hers, telegraphing his hunger as she finished knotting the rope. Desire settled like a heavy weight as he stepped off the boat. The playful urge to tease hit her and she sped off towards the house.

'Hey, where the hell are you going?' he yelled, his feet

hitting the deck behind her as he gained ground. 'Come back here.'

Catching her, he swung her round in a circle. And cut off her laugh with a kiss that promised all sorts of delicious retribution.

Her tongue tangled with his as she opened her mouth to take the kiss deeper and dug greedy fingers into his damp hair. *No more doubts, no more panicking, no more holding back,* she thought as he broke the kiss to lift her into his arms.

'Got you,' he murmured.

Euphoria slammed into her at the possessive tone.

She clung onto his neck and whispered, 'Hurry up.'

'I am hurrying, damn it,' he huffed, climbing the steps two at a time with her cradled in his arms. 'You're heavier than you used to be, pregnant lady.'

She beamed at him, impossibly pleased by the silly joke.

Everything would be okay with the baby now, because she understood where his insecurities were coming from and knew he was at least willing to try to work all those problems out.

And while they were doing that, why shouldn't they see if there could be more? He'd given her a painful glimpse into his past—had let his guard down and let her in. And she'd done the same. Her heart stuttered painfully at the thought of all the possibilities that she hadn't considered, hadn't let herself consider. She'd been so cautious up to now, mindful of Ruby's warning not to let her heart run away with itself. But was it really necessary to carry on being so careful? When they'd taken such a huge step forward today?

She clung to his shoulders and kissed the soft skin beneath his chin.

'Behave,' he growled as he staggered into the living room and headed for the stairs. 'We're not there yet.'

She laughed as he boosted her in his arms to take the stairs, the euphoria intoxicating as she imagined just how far they could go, now she was ready to take the leap.

CHAPTER ELEVEN

'YOU SMELL SO GOOD.'

Strong arms wrapped around Ella's waist from behind. She shivered as Coop nipped playfully at her ear lobe, then glared into the bathroom mirror.

'For goodness' sake, I'm trying to put my face on here.' Slicking another coat of gloss on bone-dry lips, she gave him a not exactly subtle jab with her elbow, which only made him chuckle.

'Stop freaking out, you look great.' Warm palms skimmed over the light silk of the dress she'd found in a boutique shop in Hamilton after a fraught shopping expedition yesterday, then settled on the curve of her stomach. 'How's Junior?'

A little of her aggravation dissolved, pushed out by the feel of his hands, stroking where their child grew, and the tender enquiry in his gaze as it met hers in the mirror.

'Junior's fine.' She smiled back at him. She knew he was still feeling his way, still nervous about stepping into a role he hadn't prepared for, but he'd been eager and attentive during the scan five days ago, firing questions at the obstetrician.

When the doctor had asked them if they wanted to know the sex, he'd deferred to her, but she could see how keen he was to know the answer and had decided to go with it—maybe knowing the sex would make the baby more real to him. When the doctor had pointed out their child's penis, she'd been glad she had, because she hadn't been able to stop laughing when he'd whispered with stunned delight, 'For real? The kid's hung like a horse.'

She turned in his arms, pressed her hands to his cheeks. 'But Junior's not the one who's about to meet all your friends for the first time.' She dropped a hand to her stomach, the jumpy sensation nothing to do with the child growing inside her.

Because while Coop's attitude to their child had become everything she could have hoped for, the euphoria of that day a week ago, when she'd been sure they were beginning to form a more tangible bond between the two of them, had faded considerably.

'I want them to like me,' she murmured, not quite able to keep the resentment out of her voice. She'd tried in the last week to make him understand this was important to her. And he'd resolutely refused to even meet her halfway, ignoring or deflecting her repeated requests to introduce her to anyone he knew. Just as he'd continually ignored her suggestions that she should book her flight home soon.

So here they were, on the evening of his friend's wedding, and she had no idea where she stood, not just with his friends but with him too. 'I would have preferred to at least have met some of them.'

'You already met a few of them at the Runner on our first night,' he said, in a familiar argument.

'That was four months ago!' she replied, her patience straining. 'And I hardly talked to any of them.'

'Quit panicking—they're going to love you,' he murmured, dismissing her concerns again. Lifting her hand, he pressed a kiss into the palm. 'You know what you need?'

'A Valium, maybe?' she said, only half joking.

'Nuh-uh.' One warm palm settled on her leg and then

skimmed up under her dress, to cup her buttock. 'I've got a better way to help you unwind.'

His thumb sneaked under the leg of her panties, making the pulse of heat flare, as it always did. She grasped his wrist and halted the exploration—determined not to be sidetracked again. 'Stop it, Coop. We haven't got time.'

His lips curved. 'Sure we have.' Dropping his head, he kissed the pulse point in her neck, the one place he knew from experience would drive her wild. 'You're just kind of uptight. This'll help.'

'No, it won't,' she said, but the protest trailed off as he cupped her, the heel of his palm rubbing the bundle of nerves and giving them the friction they craved.

'We can't...' She gasped, blindsided by the inevitable swelling in her sex, the rush of moisture, as one thick finger snuck past the gusset of her panties and slid over her yearning clitoris. 'I don't have time to shower again.'

'Then don't.' His clever fingers played with the swollen nub. 'I love you with that just-screwed look.'

The words registered through the haze of heat, and her temper flared. Flattening her palms against his chest, she shoved him back, shaking with frustration—and no small amount of fury. 'Get off me. How old are you, for goodness' sake?'

'What the hell are you so mad about?' He looked genuinely nonplussed. 'You want to—you know you do.'

Given that his fingers were slick, he probably thought he had a point, which only made her more mad.

Feeling the threat of tears stealing over her lids, she pushed him aside to storm out of the bathroom.

'Damn it, Ella! What the hell did I do?'

She swung round, slapping her hands on her hips, desperate to keep the anger front and centre to disguise her hurt.

'I'll tell you what you did. You never once took my feelings into account about this. If I'm nervous and uptight it's because I didn't want to go to this event not knowing anyone. I realise we're not a couple, not really, but I thought...' She blinked furiously.

She had thought what exactly? That they were a couple, that there had been something developing between them in the last few weeks that had nothing to do with their child. But how could she know that, when he was so determined to avoid anything even resembling a serious conversation?

'Of course, we're a couple,' he said grumpily, making the stab of uncertainty under her breastbone sharpen. 'We're going to this damn fiasco together, aren't we? But I still don't see why we can't make love now if we both want to.'

Because we wouldn't be making love. Or at least, you wouldn't be.

The anger and frustration collapsed inside her, consumed by anxiety. She'd leapt over the cliff days ago convinced that he would catch her. But had she jumped too soon, reading far more into his actions than was actually there?

'The reason we can't make love...' she spoke the words slowly, succinctly, willing herself not to let an ounce of her distress show '...is because we don't have the time. And I'd really rather not turn up at this wedding smelling like some woman you've just screwed.'

He swore, his expression hardening, and she thanked God for it. She'd rather deal with his temper now than risk letting him see the emotion beneath.

'That's not what I meant and you damn well know it.'

She sighed, starting to feel shaky and knowing she couldn't maintain this façade for long. 'I think we should just go, I'm sure it'll be better once I get there.'

He raked his hand through his hair, the temper disappearing as quickly as it had come—as it always did with Coop.

'Okay, I guess you're right.' He pulled his smartphone from the pocket of the dark linen trousers he'd donned for the occasion and checked the time. 'The ceremony's in thirty minutes. Josie will murder me if I'm late.'

He escorted her down the steps to the beach, as if he were handling an unexploded bomb. But as they passed his beach hut, then walked together the mile along the sand towards The Rum Runner, retracing the steps they'd taken on their first night together, he threaded his fingers through hers.

Fairy lights strung through the palm trees twinkled in the distance as the strains of music and merriment drifted towards them on the breeze. Her heart lifted at the romantic sight.

No wonder she'd fallen for Coop so fast. He was such a good man, in so many ways. Easygoing, affable, charming, energetic and always striving to do his best. Unlike Randall. But she knew he also had a host of insecurities, which he worked hard to keep hidden. Maybe his attempts to keep things casual didn't come from a lack of feeling? Perhaps he just needed a little more time? She could stay a few more days before booking her flight home.

After all, she hadn't even told him yet that her feelings had deepened, intensified. Maybe if she did...?

'I've been dreading this damn wedding ever since Josie told me about it four months ago,' he murmured, interrupting her thoughts.

'Why?' she asked, sensing his nervousness, and able at last to let go of her own. Surely meeting his friends didn't have to be bad.

'At first, I thought it was because she's still just a kid,' he said, his gaze fixed on the wedding party in the distance. 'But now I think it's the thought of promising to be with someone for the rest of your life. It spooked me. Why would anyone want to do that?'

She followed the direction of his gaze to see the beautiful young woman she'd met at his hut four months ago in the middle of the crowd of people on the beach. Her long-limbed frame was displayed to perfection in a short ivory satin gown, and her face glowed with love and excitement.

'Because they love each other? And they want to be together?' she heard herself say, willing him to believe it. 'It's not hard to make a promise to love someone if they love you in return.'

'Do you really believe that?' He glanced down at her, the look on his face remote in the fading light. 'After the number that Randall guy did on you?'

She flinched at the statement. She could have said that she had never truly loved Randall, that what she'd felt for him had been infatuation, a pale imitation of what she already felt for Coop. But the cynicism in his voice was like a body blow and she hesitated.

'Come on.' He squeezed her hand, and began to walk. 'Let's get this over with, then we can go home and do something much more interesting.'

But as he drew her towards the party the red glow of dusk and the twinkle of fairy lights didn't seem quite so romantic any more.

'So she came back?'

Coop looked up from the plate he'd been piling high with Henry's famous goat curry, to find Josie, her face radiant with love, grinning at him.

'Hey, kid. Congratulations.' He scooped her up with his free arm as she giggled and kissed his cheek. 'You look amazing,' he said as he put her down again, and she did him a twirl.

'Old enough to be getting hitched?'

'All right, you've got me there,' he admitted.

The ceremony had been several hours ago, and some-how watching her and Taylor standing together before the minister, with Ella gripping his hand to stop his fingers shaking, hadn't been as bad as he'd thought. In fact, it had been kind of touching.

Or it would have been, if listening to the wedding vows hadn't made him feel like such a jerk, for taking out his frustration on Ella when they'd been walking along the beach. He didn't know what the hell had got into him, mentioning that guy she'd dated, especially after that dumb argument they'd had back at the house.

He shouldn't have tried to jump her like that, but the truth was he'd been feeling edgy and tense for days now, ever since she'd started talking about booking a flight home, and the only time that feeling went away now was when they were making love.

'So where's Mr Josie?' he asked Josie, stifling his im-patience to get back to Ella.

He needed to chill out about her. He'd left her with Sonny and Rhona less then twenty minutes ago; she'd be good with them for a while. Sure, she'd been more subdued than usual tonight, but she was probably just tired—the kid had been restless last night and she hadn't been able to get comfortable. Once he'd got her something to eat he'd take her home and make slow, lazy love to her. And everything would be okay again.

'Taylor's over with his buddies,' Josie said wryly. 'Boasting about the swordfish he landed last week.'

'Damn, you already sound like an old married couple.' Coop chuckled.

'That's the general idea.' She smiled. 'Talking of cou-ples, why didn't you tell anyone Ella was visiting?' Josie observed, wiping the easy smile off his face.

He turned back to the buffet, the direct question unsettling him. 'Maybe I didn't want anyone bothering us,' he said, trying to inject some humour into his tone, but not quite pulling it off.

Josie's fingers touched his arm. And he glanced over his shoulder to see the serious expression on her face. Uh-oh, this couldn't be good. 'Is the baby yours, Coop?'

He dumped the plate on the table, and grasped her forearm, pulling her away from the crowd of people behind them. 'How do you know about that?' he whispered furiously.

'Because it's obvious. Especially if you know how petite she was four months ago.'

He thrust his hand through his hair. 'Damn, please tell me you haven't said anything to Ella.'

He knew she'd wanted him to tell people before she met them. If she found out they'd guessed about her condition, she'd be hurt—and that had never been his intention.

'Of course I haven't. It's not something you can bring up in a conversation with someone you've only met twice.' Josie tugged her arm out of his grasp. 'But damn, Coop, why the hell didn't you say something? If the baby's yours? Why keep it a secret? And why keep Ella's being here a secret too?'

'Because…' His mind snagged—because he'd wanted to keep things as light and non-committal as possible. Because dealing with the baby had felt like enough already. But even as the excuses sprang into his head they sounded like just that. Excuses. 'Because it's complicated,' he managed at last.

'Why is it complicated?'

'Because she lives in London,' he said, reciting the reasons he'd been giving himself for weeks, but didn't seem to fit any more. 'She's only here for a couple of weeks and it was an accident. And we hardly know each other.' Although that too didn't seem true any more.

He did know Ella: he knew how much he liked to wake up and spoon with her in the morning. How much he'd come to depend on her smile, that sunny, optimistic outlook that was so unlike his own. How addicted he'd become to her company, her enthusiasm, her bright, lively chatter about anything and everything. 'She's going to have the baby…' he paused, then soldiered on '…because we both want it.'

The admission might have surprised him, but for the rush of emotion as he recalled feeling those flutters against his palm the night before, when Ella had been snuggled against him. And seeing that tiny body on the sonogram five days ago, as the doctor had counted all his son's fingers and toes.

How had that happened? Somehow, in the last few weeks, the thing that had terrified him the most didn't terrify him any more; it excited him. He actually wanted to be a dad. But more than that, he wanted to be with Ella in a few months' time, when her body became round and heavy as it cradled their baby.

Damn, was that the reason he didn't want her to leave? It seemed so obvious now he thought about it. No wonder he got edgy every time she mentioned going back to the UK. He wanted her to have the baby, his baby, here in Bermuda. He knew he could do this thing now, and he didn't want to miss a moment of it.

'We're trying to work stuff out,' he said, seeing Josie's eyes go round with astonishment at his declaration. 'And we don't need anyone butting into our business while we're doing it.'

'Okay, I get that.' Josie nodded, surprising him. 'But I still don't see why it's that complicated, if you both want to have this baby.'

'Coop!' They both turned to see Rhona, Josie's mom, descending on them.

'Hi, Mom,' Josie answered.

Rhona fanned herself with the hat she'd been wearing during the ceremony. 'Coop, honey, I thought I should tell you, Ella went off home.'

'What? Why?' The low-level feeling of panic that had been bugging him for days resurfaced in a rush. 'Is she okay?'

'I think she's just tired.' Rhona sent him a sharp look. 'Now, don't take this the wrong way, honey, but is that girl expecting?'

Oh, hell.

'I've got to go, Rhona,' he said, ignoring Josie's muffled snort of laughter and Rhona's question before he got bombarded with a million more. He'd have a lot of explaining to do next time he saw them, but that could wait.

Bidding both women a hasty goodbye, he rushed out of the bar, and broke into a run as soon as he hit the beach.

He needed to get home, and tell Ella she didn't have to go home, that he wanted her to stay—for the baby's sake. She'd be sure to welcome the news, because she always put the baby first, and having two parents had to be better than having just one.

As he jogged up the beach steps to the house he saw the light in the bedroom window and grinned.

I love it when a plan comes together.

She was still awake. He'd tell her about his plans for their future and then they could finish what he'd been trying to start before the wedding.

'Hey, Ella,' he shouted up the stairs as he heard the whizz-bang of the fireworks Sonny had organised to finish the celebrations on the beach. Glancing over his shoulder, he caught the dazzle of light and colour as a shower of golden rain cascaded into the night sky. 'You missed the fireworks—how about we watch the display from the terrace?' He bounded up the stairs, then strode down the corridor. 'I've got something I have to tell you.'

But then he pushed the door open and spotted Ella, her arms full of silk panties, and her neatly packed suitcase laid open on the bed.

His grin flatlined as all the adrenaline that had been pumping round his system during his jog home slammed full force into his chest.

'What the hell do you think you're doing?'

CHAPTER TWELVE

ELLA WHIPPED ROUND at the surly shout, her heart jumping into her throat at the sight of Cooper, looking gorgeous and annoyed, standing in the doorway, his face cast in bold relief by the coloured lights bursting in the sky outside.

She folded her underwear into the suitcase, flipped the lid closed and took several deep breaths to slow her galloping heartbeat. 'I'm packing,' she said. 'I've booked myself on the night flight to London. It leaves at eleven.'

'What the...?' The expletive echoed round the room as he slammed the door shut. 'When exactly were you planning to tell me this? Or weren't you planning to tell me? Is that why you ran off early from the wedding?'

She stiffened, stunned by the anger, and the accusation. 'No, of course not. I planned to tell you when you got back. It's just...' She chewed on her lip, determined not to fold again under the pressure of her own insecurities. She'd let him dictate the terms of this relationship—or non-relationship—right from the start. But it was only as she'd had to stand by his side and listen to his friend recite her vows, while enduring the speculative looks of all his friends, that she'd begun to realise how little she'd been prepared to settle for. Because she had lacked the courage to demand more.

'I think we need some space,' she continued. 'There's something I have to tell you and—'

'Yeah, well, I've got something to tell you.' He cut in before she could get the words out she'd been psyching herself up to say all evening. 'I want you to stay, to move in with me.'

'What?' She sat down on the bed, her legs going bone-less as her insides tumbled with an odd combination of hope and astonishment at the unexpected offer. 'You want me to stay? Seriously?'

She hadn't been wrong: there had been something de-veloping between them, and he'd seen it too. Of course, she couldn't just abandon her life in London, but that he would even suggest such a thing had to be a very good sign that his feelings had deepened too.

He took her arm, drew her up. Touching his forehead to hers, he settled his hand on her neck, to stroke the flut-ter of her pulse. 'Of course. You're having my kid. I want to be there for you both, not thousands of miles away.'

It took a moment for her to hear the words past the de-lighted buzz of anticipation. 'But that's...' She struggled to clarify, to make sure she'd understood. 'You only want me to stay because of the baby?'

His lips quirked, his brow wrinkling in a puzzled frown. 'Yeah, of course, what else is there?'

There's me. I need you to want me too.

She stepped out of his arms, the blow both shattering and painfully ironic. When she'd first arrived in Bermuda, hearing him say those words would have felt like a miracle. But now they felt desperately bittersweet. How could she accept his offer, when she wanted so much more?

She looked into those jade-green eyes that she had come to adore, but held so many secrets, and said the only words she could. 'I can't stay, Coop. It's not—'

'Why not? Is it because of your business? I get that...' He touched her waist, trying to reassure her, but only mak-ing her heart shatter a little more. 'We can work out the logistics. I'll need to be in Bermuda for the summer season, but otherwise I can come to London. I've got money, whatever we need to do to make this work—'

'That isn't it…' She placed her hand on his cheek, loving him even more if that were possible. He was a generous man, who wanted to do the right thing for his child.

'Then what is it?' he asked.

'This isn't about the baby. It's about me, and you.'

'What?'

She swallowed, knowing she needed to tell him, and hoping against hope that he wouldn't freak out when she did. 'I think I'm falling in love with you.'

He dropped his head back to hers, let out a rush of breath and then, to her total astonishment, he chuckled, the sound deep, and amused and self-satisfied. 'Damn, is that all?'

She stepped back. 'It's not funny. I'm serious.'

He shrugged, his lips tipping in that seductive smile that she had once found so endearing. 'I know you are— so what? That's good, isn't it? If you love me you've got to stay, right?'

'Not if I don't know how you feel about me?' she heard herself say, the question in her voice making her feel needy and pathetic.

'Don't be dumb. It's obvious how I feel about you. I like having you around.' He held her waist, tugged her back into his arms. 'I've invited you to move in, haven't I? At least until the kid's born.'

She braced her hands on his chest, hearing the qualification. 'But that's not enough.'

His brow furrowed. 'Why not?'

'Because I need more than that. You're asking me to make a major change in my life, to move thousands of miles away from everything I know on what sounds like a whim.' The emotion clogged in her throat at the look of total confusion on his face.

'What do you want me to say? That I love you? Is that it?' The bitter edge in his tone made the traitorous tears she'd refused to shed sting her eyes. 'If you need me to say the words I will.'

'This isn't about words.' She drew back. 'It's about emotions. It's about you being honest with me about your feelings.'

Coop stared at Ella's earnest expression, saw the glitter of tears in those trusting blue eyes and felt the panic that he had kept at bay ever since his mother's death start to choke him.

He didn't do emotion, he didn't even talk about it, because it reminded him too much of the deep, dark, inescapable hole where he'd spent most of his childhood.

'You don't know what you're asking,' he said, desperately bartering for time, scrambling around for a way to avoid the conversation. 'I'm not good at that stuff.'

'I know that, Coop.' She sighed, the sound weary and so full of despair it cut right through his heart. 'And I understand. I took a huge knock to my confidence too when Randall rejected me. If I hadn't, it wouldn't have taken me so long to tell you all this. But you have to understand. I can't come and live with you, bring up a child with you and all the time live in some kind of weird limbo where you get to call all the shots because—' she lifted her fingers to do air quotes '—you're "not good at this stuff".' She stood up, brushed her hands down her dress in a nervous gesture he recognised. 'I need to call a cab.'

She turned to pick up her case from the bed. He dived ahead of her, gripped the handle. 'You don't need a cab. You're not going tonight.'

She blinked, the sheen of tears crucifying him. 'Yes, I

am. I have to go. I'm tired and we both need space, maybe once—'

'Don't go.' His voice cracked on the word. 'It's not that I don't want to talk about it, it's that I can't.'

'Why can't you?' she asked, the tone gentle but probing, scraping at the raw wound he'd thought had healed years before.

'Because I'll mess it up. Because I'll say the wrong thing, or I'll say it in the wrong way. They're just words— they don't mean anything. What matters is what we do, not what we say to each other.'

She nodded, but he could see the concern in her gaze, and felt as if she was looking through the veneer of charm and confidence and seeing the frightened little boy cowering beneath. 'Coop, whatever made you think that there's a wrong and a right answer?'

She laid a palm on his cheek, but he jerked back. Terrified of being drawn into that dark place again.

'You say that, but there is a right answer. If there wasn't I wouldn't have given her the wrong one. I told her I loved her, that I could look after her, but it didn't change a thing.'

She watched him, her unwavering gaze so full of the love he knew he wasn't capable of giving back, all the panic imploded inside him until all that was left was the pain.

'Who are you talking about, Coop?'

His heart hammered his ribs as he dropped his chin, fisted his fingers to stop them shaking and murmured, 'My mom.'

Ella stared, unable to speak around the lump wedged in her throat. She could see the painful shadow of memory in his expression, and wished she could take it away. Reaching for his hand, she folded her fingers around his and held on. 'Can you tell me about her?'

He cleared his throat, but he didn't pull his hand out of hers. 'There's not a lot to tell. She had an affair with my old man, he gave her the standard line about leaving his wife. And she got pregnant with me, before she figured out he was lying.'

'He sounds like a very selfish person,' Ella said, then remembered how he'd once compared himself to his father. 'And nothing like you.'

'Thanks.' He sent her a half-smile, but it did nothing to dispel the shadow in his eyes. 'Anyway, he wasn't interested in me, but he carried on screwing my mom from time to time, so she convinced herself he loved her.' He shrugged, but the movement was stiff and tense, and she knew he was nowhere near as relaxed as the gesture suggested.

She pressed her hand to his chest, desperate to soothe the frantic beats of his heart. 'You don't have to tell me any more, if it upsets you. I understand.' His mother had obviously fallen in love with a man who had used her and carried on using her. Was it any wonder that after witnessing that throughout the years of his childhood, he'd be cynical about love himself? And wary about making any kind of commitment. 'I shouldn't have pushed you. It wasn't fair.'

'Yeah, you should have.' He covered her hand. 'And I don't think you do get it, Ella.' He sighed. 'The thing is, she was so fragile. She wanted something she couldn't have and she had these dark moods because she couldn't cope with that. At first, when I was really little, she'd have the odd day when she couldn't get out of bed, and she'd just cry and want to hug me. But as I got older, it got worse and worse, until she couldn't hold down a job. I tried to make things better for her. As soon as I was old enough, I got a job. I figured if I could make enough money...' He stared into the darkness, the hopelessness on his face devastating. 'But I couldn't. Whatever I did, whatever I said, it was never the right thing.'

'Coop,' she murmured, desperate to try and take the hopelessness away. 'It sounds as if she suffered from depression. Money can't cure that.' Or a child's devotion.

'I know, but…'

She leant into him, the love welling up her chest as he looped his arm round her shoulders. 'What happened to her?'

She heard him swallow, the sound loud in the stillness of the night. 'I came home from the graveyard shift at the drive-thru one night and found her in the bathroom. She'd taken too many of the pills she used to sleep. I called the paramedics, but it was too late.'

Ella pulled back, the tears soaking her lashes. 'I'm so sorry that you found her like that.' And that he'd had such a bleak childhood. No wonder he'd been so determined to protect himself—he'd suffered so much, at such a young age. 'But surely you must see that you weren't to blame. Whatever you said or didn't say, it wouldn't have made a difference.'

'Hey, don't cry.' He scooped the tear off her lashes. 'And I guess you're right. But that's not the reason I didn't want to tell you about her.'

She swallowed down the tears. 'So what is?'

'I didn't want you to know what a coward I am.'

'A coward?' She didn't understand: he'd done his best; he'd stuck by his mother and tried so hard to make her life easier, better. 'How can you say that when you did everything you could for her?'

'Maybe I did. But I'm not talking about her. I'm talking about us.' His lips tipped up in a wry smile. 'The thing is, even though I loved my mom, and I was sad when she died…' he gave his head a small shake '…you know what I felt most when I stood by her graveside?'

She shook her head, confused now. What was he trying to tell her?

'Relief.' The word came out on a huff of breath. 'I was
so damn glad I didn't have to be responsible for her any
more.' He cupped her cheek, brushing the tears off her
lashes. 'For years after her death, I used to have this re-
curring nightmare that I was standing by her grave and
her hand would come out and drag me in with her. Because that's what it felt like when I was growing up, being
trapped in this big dark hole that I could never get out of.
So I ran and I kept on running. Once I landed here, I devoted myself to making money, until I had enough to make
the nightmares go away. But I never realised until this moment that in a lot of ways I never stopped running.' His
hand stroked down to rest on her stomach.

'I'm sorry that I didn't tell everyone about you, and
the baby. And that I'm not good with stuff like this. But if
you'll just give me another chance, I'll try not to be such
a damn coward again. Because I don't want to keep running any more.'

She stared at him, her heart bursting with happiness and
giddy relief. Maybe it wasn't a declaration of undying and
everlasting love. But she'd had one of those before and it
had been a lie. Coop's declaration meant so much more.

'I think maybe we both need to stop being cowards,'
she said. 'I should have had the guts to tell you straight
away that my feelings were changing, that I wanted more,
instead of panicking about how you would react.'

His hands framed her face, to pull her gaze back to his,
and the approval she saw there was as intoxicating as the
heat. 'You were just scared. Believe me, I get that. Just so
long as you're not scared any more?'

She bobbed her head in answer to his question, far too
emotional to speak.

'Cool.' He wrapped his arms round her waist, the solid

feel of him making heat eddy up from her core to add to the joy.

She threaded her hands through the short hair above his ears, tugged his head down to hers and poured out everything she felt for him in a kiss full of happiness and desire and the rush of emotion that no longer had to be denied.

When they finally came up for air, he cradled her cheeks. 'So will you cancel your flight? I know you've got to go home soon, but when you do I'd like to come too, until we figure out how we're going to work this out. I'm not good at making promises. But I know I want to be with you, not just because of the baby, but because…' He ducked his head, swore softly under his breath, the flags of embarrassed colour on his cheeks sweet and endearing and impossibly sexy. 'Hell, I'm pretty damn sure I'm falling for you, too.'

She laughed, the sound rich and throaty and full of hope as she clung onto his neck. 'All right, but only on one condition.'

The quick grin on his lips sparkled with a heady combination of tenderness and wickedness. 'Seriously, you've got another condition? That's pushing it.'

'I'll stay on the condition that I get to give you that just-screwed look I adore.'

He laughed. 'Yup, definitely pushing it.'

He was still chuckling when he dumped her on the bed a few minutes later and got to work giving her what she wanted.

EPILOGUE

'THAT WATER IS so warm, it's incredible,' Ruby said as she reached for one of the beach towels and patted herself dry.

Ella shielded her eyes against the sun to smile at her friend from her spot on the lounger. 'I know, but we should probably call the guys in soon, or we're going to have some very cranky kids on our hands later.'

Ruby turned towards the sea, her smile crafty. 'Yes, but they are going to sleep like the dead, once their fathers have put them to bed.'

Ella laughed, her gaze following Ruby's out to the shallow surf, where Cooper and Ruby's husband Callum were busy playing some kind of splashing war with their children. Cal ran forward, with his four-year-old Arturo clamped to his back like a limpet, while his daughter Ally shouted instructions and charged by his side. Her older brother Max seemed to be in cahoots with Cooper, who had their two-year-old son Jem slung on his hip, as he and Max launched a new offensive against the Westmore invaders. Jem's delighted chuckles were matched by the manic pumping of his little legs as his Daddy scooped up a tidal wave of water with his free arm and drenched Ally, Cal and Arturo in one fell swoop.

Ella grinned at the comical scene as Max began to do a victory dance.

She loved having Ruby and Cal and their family visiting them in Bermuda for the summer—especially now that she and Cooper had made the decision to move here permanently and sell the flat Coop had bought in Camden just before Jem's birth. It had been a major wrench finally agreeing to let that part of her life go, not least because she knew she would miss her best friend terribly, but as Jem got older they'd decided that jetting backwards and forwards between their two home bases was too confusing for him—and getting him over the jet lag every few months nothing short of a nightmare.

'Do the daddies know they're on bedtime duty?' Ella asked as the splashing war went into a new phase, Ally, Cal and Arturo apparently refusing to concede defeat. She suspected both men were going to be even more exhausted than the kids come bedtime if the war carried on much longer.

Ruby settled on the sun lounger next to her and sent her a wicked grin. 'They won't have a choice when I tell them you and I still have lots of important business to conduct concerning the new Touch of Frosting opening in Hamilton.'

'But I thought we got everything sorted yesterday?' Ella said, remembering the fabulous brainstorming session they'd had discussing recipes and displays for the opening of her new bakery in two weeks' time, which Ruby and her family were staying to attend.

'Yes, but they don't know that, do they?'

Ella laughed. 'Ruby, you're nasty.'

'I try,' Ruby replied, smiling back. Then she reached over to take Ella's hand, her smile becoming hopeful. 'So, Ella, you've been so upbeat, I'm assuming you got good news from the specialist last week?'

Ella gripped her friend's fingers, and let the moment of melancholy pass before replying. Ruby knew she and Coop had been trying for another child for over a year, so of course she would ask. 'Actually, it wasn't the news we wanted.'

Ruby sat upright, her smile disappearing. 'Ella, I'm so sorry. I shouldn't have brought it up, I just assumed...'

'No, that's okay.' She tugged Ruby's hand to reassure her. 'Really, it is. We knew it was a long shot.' She allowed her gaze to drift over to her two precious guys, still playing like loons together in the surf with the Westmores, and the smile that was never far away returned. 'It would be incredibly selfish of me to expect another miracle in my life.' She paused, the smile getting bigger. 'After the two I already have.'

Because she considered Coop to be as much of a miracle as their baby. He'd rescued her, she thought, in so many ways, and she'd rescued him. They had both found something wonderful together, not just in Jem but with each other, something made even more wonderful by the fact that they hadn't even realised it had been missing from their lives until they'd found it.

'Even so,' Ruby said, 'it seems such a shame it should be so hard for you to have more children when you make such incredible parents.'

'I know,' she said, not caring if the statement sounded a little smug. 'Which is why we're thinking of becoming foster parents.'

'You are?' Ruby's smile returned. 'That sounds like a great idea.'

'We think so. It's early days yet, but we're both excited about it. Cooper runs free snorkelling classes at the marina for kids with...' she paused '...challenging home situations.' Something he knew far too much about himself. 'Anyway, one of the social workers who escorts the kids suggested it to him—because she's seen how well he handles them. So we've started the ball rolling. There's a lot of paperwork and we have to do a...'

The sound of a toddler's crying reached them, interrupting Ella's enthusiastic reply. She sat up, seeing her husband strolling towards her across the sand, with Jem clinging to his neck and rubbing his eyes—his little head drenched in seawater.

'Oh, dear, what happened?' she said as they approached, trying not to smile, Jem looked so forlorn.

'We had to retire from the field,' Coop announced, casting a stern eye at Ruby. 'Thanks to a sneaky stealth attack from Super-Splash-Girl.'

'I should have warned you.' Ruby smiled, handing Coop a towel to wipe Jem's face. 'Ally takes no prisoners, and she always plays to win. I'm afraid it's the curse of having two brothers.'

'Want ice cream, Daddy,' Jem wailed as if he'd just undergone an extreme form of water torture.

'OK, buddy.' Coop handed Ruby back the towel. 'I guess you earned one.' He rubbed his son's back as the small head drooped onto his shoulder. 'As well as a lecture on the wiles of women.'

Ruby chuckled. 'Good luck with that.'

'Do you want me to take him?' Ella asked, reaching for the exhausted child.

'Nah, he's good. I'll see if I can sneak a scoop of strawberry past Inez, then I'll put him down for his nap.' Holding his son securely against his chest, he leant down to press a kiss to her lips, whispering as he drew back, 'Then maybe we can have *our* afternoon nap?'

The heat sizzled happily down to her core as she caressed her son's damp blond curls and grinned up at her extremely hot husband. 'Possibly, as long as I don't have to listen to a lecture on the wiles of women.'

'No problem.' He winked. 'I've got a whole other lecture planned for you, sweetheart.'

Saying goodbye to Ruby, he headed towards the beach steps up to the house.

Ella studied his broad tanned back, the muscular, capable shoulder where her drowsy son's head was securely cradled, and then let her gaze drift down to the wet board shorts clinging to tight buns.

She let out a contented sigh as her happiness combined with the hum of heat. While her husband would still rather have his teeth pulled than talk about his feelings—when it came to lectures in bed, she'd never been able to fault his energy, enthusiasm… Or his expertise.

* * * * *

If you want to read Ruby and Cal's story, look for CUPCAKES AND KILLER HEELS by Heidi Rice available on Harlequin.com on eBook.